ACROSS THE BRIDGE

A Rikers Island Story

Steven Dominguez

Cover illustrated by: Richard Parker
Instagram: @Maderich

Molding Messengers

A Molding Messengers Publication

Across the Bridge a Rikers Island Story

For information about permission to reproduce selections from this book, Write to Molding Messengers, LLC 1728 NE Miami Gardens Dr, Suite #111, North Miami Beach, FL 33179 or email Info.Staff@MoldingMessengers.com

Library of Congress Control Number: 2020952345

Print ISBN: 978-0-578-82654-7
eBook ISBN: 978-0-578-82655-4

Molding Messengers

A Molding Messengers Publication

ACROSS THE BRIDGE

A Rikers Island Story

Steven Dominguez

Cover illustrated by: Richard Parker
Instagram: @Maderich

Molding Messengers

A Molding Messengers Publication

ACKNOWLEDGEMENTS

THE EVENTS DEPICTED HEREIN ARE BASED ON A FIGMENT OF MY PERSONAL JOURNEY AND MY INDIVIDUAL PERCEPTION, WHILE A NYC CORRECTION OFFICER. CHARACTERS AND PLACES HAVE BEEN ALTERED TO PROTECT THE INNOCENT. A SMALL PERCENTAGE OF THESE ACTIONS HAVE BEEN SLIGHTLY FABRICATED TO GIVE THE WORK OF ART A SENSE OF RAW REALITY AND TO PROMOTE ENTERTAINMENT.

THIS TRANSCRIPT IS DEDICATED TO EVERYONE WHO HAS FOUND THEMSELVES IN A PREDICAMENT OF "DOING SOMETHING WRONG FOR THE 'RIGHT' REASON". WHICH IS EXACTLY WHAT I DID. WHEN THE SYSTEM FAILS YOU, YOU TEND TO CREATE YOUR OWN. I REPETITIOUSLY DISREGARDED THE LAW WHILE ATTEMPTING TO UPHOLD IT.

THIS BOOK IS ALSO DEDICATED TO EVERYONE AND ANYONE INCARCERATED, FACING TRAIL, JUST STARTING, IN THE MIDDLE, OR AT THE END OF THEIR BID. FOR EVERYONE 'BEHIND THE WALL', EVERYONE

WHO DID'NT RECEIVE A LETTER OR A VISIT TODAY. TO EVERYONE WHO'S BATTLED A MENTAL ILLNESS OR STRUGGLING WITH INTEGRITY.

ASK YOURSELF, "IS THE RISK WORTH YOUR LIFESTYLE?" THEN FOLLOW THAT QUESTION WITH "IS THIS LIFESTYLE WORTH YOUR FREEDOM?" NEVER SELL YOUR SOUL TO MAKE A DOLLAR. I KNOW WE GREW UP HOPELESS BUT YOU GOTTA STAY FOCUSED.

MAY THE SOULS OF KHALIEF BROWDER, LAYLEEN CUBILETTE-POLANCO, JEROME MURDOIGH, NICHOLAS FELICIANO, JASON ECHEVARRIA, CARINA MONTES, JOSE CRUZ, REST IN PEACE.

LAST BUT NOT LEAST, THANK YOU, MOM. MY GRANDPARENTS FOR ALL THE JEWELS YA PROVIDED ME. THANK YOU TO MY FRIENDS & LOVED ONES THAT ASSISTED IN MY SANITY. I LOVE & MISS YOU STEVEN RODRIGUEZ (ASAP YAMS) THIS FOR YOU.

WHAT I CAN'T PAYBACK TO YOU ALL,
GOD WILL.

CHAPTER 1

Julissa takes a drag of her cigarette.

"I really can't wait to see you!" Julissa holds the phone tight between her ear and her shoulder. She continues to stir the pasta in the boiling pot of water. A gruff, yet charming, voice responds on the other end of the phone.

"Me, too, girl," Dollar says. "I hate this shit. You still got me though, right?"

"Oh, my God. Yes! Shut up already!" Julissa playfully confirms as she strains the steaming hot pasta into another bowl.

"Who the fuck you yelling at? Watch when I see you tonight, bitch!" Dollar jokes.

Julissa carefully layers each sheet of pasta into the Pyrex dish and spoons generous amounts of ricotta cheese between each layer. On the other end of the phone Dollar continues to playfully flirt with her. She places the dish into the oven and proceeds into her bedroom to get dressed for work. She wears tight-fitting navy-blue cargo pants with heavy military-style boots and slips on a fitted white tee. The rest of her uniform is hung up neatly in her locker at work.

"Babe, you know I got you. I'll see you soon," she pauses, "I love you, boo."

Dollar's fellow inmates carry on gambling, smoking, watching TV, and politicking. In a low and impatient voice, he responds, "Yeah, ok. Love you too."

They hang up the phone and Dollar walks back towards the group of men. He snatches the remote and changes the channel. No one risks speaking up.

Julissa, ready for work, uses a spatula to carve out a large portion of lasagna and places it into Tupperware. She lifts a few layers of the dish and places a carefully wrapped package of uncut heroin in between the pasta, then pours sauce over the entire dish. She packs the Tupperware with the rest of her lunch and heads downstairs.

Julissa crosses the street towards her parked car as locals gawk in her direction. She struts what she has and walks with the utmost confidence, clutching her personal firearm on the left of her hip. A group of guys are posted by her luxury car.

"Get your asses off my fucking car!" she shouts.

The young men laugh and walk off. They don't want any problems. Everyone in the neighborhood knows what she does for a living. She's strapped and has the legal right to use it. She pops her trunk and throws in her duffle bag, quickly scrolling through her phone.

"I have on the job training, 11pm-7am. Can I catch a ride with you tonight?" a text message sent 15 minutes ago from her cousin Antonio.

She calls him. It rings twice and Antonio's voice answers with joy.

"Hey, Ju!" he greets.

"I could've sworn you didn't start until this coming Monday!" Julissa retorts confused.

"No, my academy instructor said we go in tonight, thank goodness. I lucked out being assigned to the same facility you work at."

"Wow! Um. Ok, be outside in ten minutes. And you better be ready, I hate being late for the overnight shift," she directs.

She presses the push-to-start button of her Mercedes and speeds her way towards him. He lives four avenues down from her. A 5-minute drive if that. At the red light she spots Antonio, 21-year-old Latino male, tall and slender, a baby-faced young man with a disarming smile. He is by the bus stop patiently awaiting her arrival and dressed in full correction officer uniform. Julissa beeps her horn from the opposite corner, signaling him to run to her while the light remains red. Her luxury car glistens under the street lights.

He jumps in, all smiles, and gives her a kiss on her cheek. "Perfect timing, right?!" he lightly shouts, clearly excited.

She looks at him from top to bottom, astonished. "Tony! Are you fucking crazy? You can't be out here in full uniform. You need to be more discreet! You have no personal firearm or anything!" she yells at the top of her smoke-filled lungs. He puts on his seatbelt as she stares at his innocence. The light turns green and they speed off.

When they pull up, the giant illuminated sign reads "DEPARTMENT OF CORRECTIONS - RIKERS ISLAND - HOME OF NEW YORK CITY'S BOLDEST."

"Take out your badge and ID!" she reminds him.

They both display their credentials to the officer sitting inside the booth. He dismisses them with a peace sign.

It's 10:30PM, yet it seems to get darker as they drive over the bridge. The window remains rolled down and the muggy smell of waste from the neighboring power plant fills the island's air. To Antonio's right is LaGuardia

Airport. He watches as a Boeing 747 plane fly directly over them, too close over them for his comfort. So much is going through his mind as he sees the jail get closer and closer. The bridge, even though not steep, gives him a rollercoaster feel. It's the nerves.

"Damn. Is it normal to feel nervous?" he questions, "My anxiety is through the roof."

"Don't worry, that's typical. My first few days were very difficult. Just be yourself, be on point, and always be aware of your surroundings," Julissa asserts.

They get across the bridge and look for a parking space in a parking lot full of lavish vehicles, more lavish than he expected. The place is packed with recently hired officers, just like him, preparing for their new journeys. They bypass a second booth designated for department transportation buses and official department vehicles. Julissa earned a Gate One pass that allows her to drive straight to her command facility and not have to park further out or depend on the shuttle buses most officers and other staff take. Antonio has been quiet and still the entire ride.

She parks directly in front of G.M.D.C., also known as C-73, one of seven operating buildings on Rikers that houses male adult inmates only. They both enter and walk through the metal detectors that the staff is required to clear in order to proceed. Antonio catches a whiff of new paint, dirt, grime, rust, and chemicals. He looks around the dimly lit building and warship gray walls.

It's 11:00PM and two rows of about 26 correction officers await their assignments, standing along the wall to the main corridor outside the central control room where all keys, radios, pepper sprays, tactical gear, log books, and other equipment are for which officers can sign. Everyone quiets down while Captain Karen Mitchell debriefs. She is a busty African American woman in her late 30s with hazel eyes. It is evident that she wears pride for being a captain, and it is known that she takes advantage of her position when needed.

"My 11-7 tour, standby after names and assigned post are called. I have training officers accompanying some of you tonight! Teach them correctly, thank you!" she shouts.

The senior correction officers roll their eyes and suck their teeth in disappointment. They know that instead of a normal semi-quiet night like they are used to, they will be rudely interrupted by new officers asking questions and disrupting their nap, which most get to enjoy once everyone settles.

Captain Mitchell continues, "Mason & OJT Green, 7 main! Mack & Richards, dorm 10! Sanchez & Sanchez, staff kitchen!"

Antonio grins proudly as he hears that he's paired with his cousin. When roll call breaks, he bee-lines towards Julissa and the other officers mingle. A couple of male correction officers prowl on the young rookie female training officers, pointing out the vulnerable ones they plan on spitting game to once they acclimate.

"That's a crazy coincidence, right?" Antonio tells his cousin.

Julissa smiles and weakly steps close to Captain Mitchell in the corner. She leans into the podium, "Thanks girl. I owe you big time." Julissa is referring to a side favor that Captain Mitchell asked for a few days prior.

"Don't sweat it, you'll need me again," Captain Mitchell retorts.

They give one another a seductive stare as Antonio stands firm and within earshot of their conversation, waiting for instructions. Julissa walks off in a sexual stroll poking out her backside. The officers slowly make their way to their post, some gathering keys and radios; others walk toward the staff kitchen to place their lunch in the refrigerator. Julissa nods to Antonio to follow her exactly there.

"So, what's the game plan?" Antonio questions with a huge smile.

"Look Tony, this tour is a relaxed shift. We barely work hard right now. All we need to do is gather my inmate workers to clean throughout the night, and also prepare breakfast for 5am chow. Grab a few snacks from the vending machine for the both of us. I pulled strings so that you would be with me tonight."

Digging into his pockets for loose change, Antonio looks around and an amplifying sound from bells goes off, emergency sirens follow as an officer's departmental radio screeches.

Loud speakers / radios simultaneously sound off. Officers run towards the location of roll call to gather their riot gear and put on their helmets.

Warden Kenneth Brown, a mid-50s, Caucasian male sporting a salt and pepper military haircut steps out of his office and heads towards the central control room, reaching for his walkie-talkie as officers breeze by him responding to the alarm. Someone in the central control office shouts on the radio.

"10-11! 10-11! IN PROGRESS!" the voice on the radio screams, "ALL AVAILABLE STAFF, REPORT TO THE STAGING AREA!"

Antonio and other rookie training officers stand by startled.

"Oh, my goodness! Stand by, Tony!" Julissa tells Antonio, evidently pissed off.

Captain Mitchell is at the gate and requests that her favorite officer, Julissa, be in charge of recording this whole ordeal, "Grab the camera please! We have multiple inmates! Dorm 12, let's go!"

All alarms require a wave of officers, including a captain, to tend to the affected area and to always record the process from the moment the officers suit up in riot gear to the time they arrive at the scene of incident, for liability and security purposes. That way the inmates can't file false accounts of what transpired, and the same goes for the officers. Being on camera can save your career, but also damage it.

Julissa unlocks the camera box and puts on her riot gear. She follows the first wave of four correction officers jogging with their wooden bamboo batons in hand, making their way towards the area of incident. The handheld camera held directly in front of her riot helmet. Chemical agents utilized by the housing area officer cause the response team to cough profusely through their helmets, along with the inmates involved. Inmates attempt to seek refuge amidst the chaos. Officers restrain them one by one, detaining the aggressors by using the plastic flex handcuffs. Blood with a mix of hot water covers the entrance of the dorm where an inmate was slashed while on a phone call.

"Get on the fucking ground! Now!" a random correction officer yells to all the inmates.

Captain Mitchell gets on the departmental radio and calls for an update to the central control room. She presses the side button, "Central control, be advised we have six packages involved, one in need of medical attention stat! I'm in route to the main clinic. Permission to stand down from the alarm while housing officers lock down the dorm?" she asks the Warden.

"10-4. Proceed with those packages and prepare for inmate decontamination then 10-2 me upon arrival to the main clinic. Is that a copy?"

"That's a 10-4 sir!" Captain Mitchell nods.

The four suited officers escort the inmates through the corridor and up the stairs towards the clinic. The sirens in the hallway are still red indicating an alarm still in progress. They each enter one officer and one inmate at a time, strategically separating them all. The medical staff makes space available for incoming inmates. It's 12am, which is usually a fairly quiet time for the clinic, since most of the population is locked in. The dorm side is the open range. Inmates are allowed to walk to the bathroom at any given time, giving ample opportunity to cause ruckus, especially when the lights are off in the common areas.

"Yo, whatever house you land in next, make sure you tell the bros to get ready. This isn't over!" a random inmate holds his busted lip and bloody nose as he yells to his other comrades.

The inmates commence the decontamination process via sprays at designated water faucets. One of the inmates starts trembling, holding the bloody side of his face with a towel.

Doctor Lau, a short Asian male in his early 40s, annoyed and sleepy, tends to the victim with the open gash across his face and neck. He shakes his head. Even though he's seen this event over a thousand times in his career, he is always taken aback at how severe or brutal a slashing can be.

"Sir, let me see the damage so I can disinfect and patch you up, ok?" Doctor Lau pleads.

Captain Mitchell walks towards them both, “Didn’t I just move you yesterday? What happened?” she questions the wounded inmate in disappointment.

Julissa returns the camera and takes off her helmet and vest along with the other responsive officers. It’s the start of a long night for most of them. They all know how to write incident and injury reports, and possible infractions with which to serve the inmates for disorderly conduct and assault charges. Something that could ultimately land them all in the box. Julissa walks back to the staff kitchen remembering she left not only her lunch but Antonio there as well.

Antonio speed walks towards his cousin Julissa, “Are you okay? What just happened?” he asks her with concern.

“Nothing too crazy, Crip gang member. They're not too liked on the dorm side of the building. Have you seen my bags? I have infractions and incident paperwork to do, since I held the camera. Let’s go before this shit goes off again,” she leads the way.

They exit the staff break room descending through the kitchen.

Inside the dorm housing area, it's lights out and inmate Dollar walks towards the A-station bubble office, which is a small office that is located in the middle of a housing area with a solid visual of the unit. Correction Officer Janet Johnson, a loud and obnoxious mid-40s African American woman, is on the phone, nonchalantly painting her nails.

"Ms. J, what's up with Ms. Sanchez? Do you think I'm still going to work?" Dollar quietly whispers through the Plexiglas separating them.

"She should be on her way, Parker. There was an alarm not too long ago so give it a few," CO Johnson informs him.

He paces back and forth frustrated. The door buzzes open, letting Antonio and Julissa into the dorm housing area. Dollar steps out visibly disgusted and annoyed. He glances at Antonio.

"Should I frisk and search him?" Antonio quickly asks.

"Frisk?!" Dollar exclaims.

"No, he's good. He's my senior worker," Julissa defends, "Ms. Johnson we'll be back before the next count."

Johnson nods, continuing her far more important phone conversation full of gossip. She buzzes them all out of the dorm without a care in the world. They all step out into the corridor.

"Ms. Sanchez, where did they pop off at? I bet it was dorm 12!" Dollar asks concerned.

"Yeah.... Wait, how did you know?" Julissa raises an eyebrow.

They both laugh while Antonio stares him up and down lagging behind them. His body language shows his discomfort with how laid back she is with this inmate. He can sense something funny is going on as they converse about miscellaneous topics, heading towards the back entrance of the kitchen and passing all the metal detectors. They arrive through the back door of the kitchen where a couple of other inmates power wash the machines and start to clean. Julissa and Antonio sit inside the bubble office. Dollar puts on his headphones, turns on his radio, goes straight to a few of his boys, and picks up a broom.

"I'll be right back, too, Tony. Bathroom then lunch bag," Julissa tells him.

He gives her thumbs up, watching her walk out towards Dollar. He locks eyes with him delivering a smirk back. Julissa waves her hand at Dollar, signaling him to head her direction. He sweeps a path and maneuvers around the heavy machinery and sinks.

"What's up with you, bitch? And who the fuck is that clown with you?" Dollar whispers with aggression.

"He's my cousin. Chill the fuck out! Take this and act like you're going to throw it out in the garbage, move!" she looks back to check if Tony is paying attention. Julissa hands over the small Tupperware from her see-through plastic bag. It's still fairly hot. "I didn't know I had to babysit tonight. I'm sorry. Call me tomorrow afternoon, I'm working a double," she reminds him.

He shrugs her off shaking his head in amazement.

"You're so fucking ungrateful. Wow," she whispers.

"You're a crazy bitch, Juju. Word," Dollar mumbles.

Dollar steps out her way. She enters the staff bathroom and slams the door behind her. Dollar sees Antonio watching the whole interaction from the officer's bubble. He disrespectfully waves and bursts out laughing. Antonio cannot believe what he just witnessed his cousin do.

CHAPTER 2

It's 6:55AM and the cars, buses, and delivery trucks are exiting and entering the Rikers Island bridge. Planes departing and ascending, across the water, on the tarmac at LaGuardia Airport which sits just below the sunrise. It's a busy morning like always. Inmates being transported to court, the 7am-3pm officers coming in to start their shift, the 11pm-7am leaving. There is a lot of traffic on the bridge as there is only one lane for exiting and entering.

Captain Mitchell leaves work in a rush to get home after working an almost 17hr shift. She grabs her phone and calls her boyfriend, "Sean, I am running a little late! Please have Leah ready with her lunch and snack for school. I'll call you when I am outside so you can bring her down."

"I already know, man! Shut up!" Sean angrily responds.

Sean is a 30-year-old Jamaican-American low life with a shady past. He and Captain Mitchell have a 9-year-old daughter together. Sean watches TV in her apartment and takes a puff of his blunt. Their Daughter Leah remains sound asleep on the couch to the right of him.

An oncoming delivery truck flies into Captain Mitchell's direction and T- bones her car. Glass shatters. Airbags deploy. She's unconscious at the intersection.

At the bus stop nearby, Mya, a tall fully-developed Latina teenager with long, dirty blonde hair, has just witnessed the terrible car accident. She had just been debating whether she should attend class or take the bus to visit her boyfriend who's currently housed on Rikers. Her cell phone rings. She answers.

"You have a collect call from…" the operator informs her from the other side of the phone.

She presses 1, bypassing the automated message, "Hey, babe! Yes or No?" Mya frantically questions as she watches the bus try to dodge the ambulance and accident in the middle of the intersection.

"Yeah, pull up. Just be careful and please don't fuck this up either!" a raspy voice on the other line asserts.

"Okay! I'm getting on the bus once they clear up this accident. It looks like it was an officer that was driving, too," she tells him.

Ambulances, medics, and other emergency personnel in the background tend to the collision. Mya enters the Q100 bus and reaches for her metro card.

The visitor registration building opens its doors. Officers set up x-ray machines and hand wands, preparing for a busy visitor morning. CO Jones, a mixed-race, 28-year-old ladies' man, sits in a corner enjoying his breakfast sandwich and protein shake, scrolling through his phone. He gets a message.

"On the bus to see you know who…hopefully you're working today and I see you too! *heart emoji* *kiss emoji*"

He smiles and places his phone inside the pocket of his stab-resistant vest. If he gets caught with his cell phone again, his good looks will no longer make him an exception to him being written up. The officers quickly attend a small roll call and debriefing.

Warden Brown stands behind the podium with a militant stance, pointing his right index finger in the air to gather the attention of his staff members who whisper amongst one another before starting their shift.

"Good morning. I cannot stress enough how much endless tension this occupation may bring, along with overtime that seems to be never ending. Captain Mitchell was in an accident shortly after her tour this morning, right out by the entrance to the bridge. Please be more cautious. Rest in between shifts, if possible, and stay hydrated.

Temperatures are going to reach 90 degrees today," Warden Brown's words are compassionate.

Officers look at one another, shocked by the news.

"Medical staff has informed me that she will be okay, but she did suffer a broken shoulder and a concussion. There will be a donation envelope going around as she'll need to be out of work for a few months," Warden continues, "Lastly, have a safe tour and watch each other's backs."

Roll call breaks. Julissa walks over, tapping the Warden on the shoulder, "I really hope she's okay," Julissa uneasily tells him.

He gazes at her with the utmost seriousness, "Sanchez, you know more than many how much overtime she does. On top of her alcohol intake, I don't know. They might not administer a breathalyzer, but we'll see. Call me later and I will keep you posted. I plan on visiting her at the hospital with a couple of union representatives for moral and legal support in a few hours."

She stares blank and teary-eyed. He walks away. Julissa steps out to light a cigarette as Antonio walks out of the staff locker room. He tails her through the front gate. Other than the alarm and that awkward transaction between his cousin and that inmate, it was a pretty decent night. He gets to go home since job training officers don't get overtime.

They stand in front of the C-73 building facing the parking lot.

"Guess I'll see you tonight?" Antonio reminds Julissa.

Caught in a daze her response is awkwardly delayed, "Yep, I'll be here. I practically live here it seems like," she slowly responds.

CO Jones steps out to the front entrance lighting his cigarette as the employee route bus stops directly in front of them. Correction officers exit the bus with female civilians who quickly greet and flirt with him.

"Damn. You got all the juice, huh?" Julissa playfully says.

Jones gives her a friendly shove and they laugh it out.

Inside of the cells side of the building that houses inmates with more serious charges, there are inmates doing pushups, inmates on the phone, and inmates who are watching TV. Shorty, Latino male in his early 20s with French braids and a napoleon complex, stands a good 5 feet flat. He steps into his cell as another inmate stands by the sliding door. He sits on his bed putting together a piece of saran wrap and lotion.

"I hope this bitch doesn't fumble bro," Shorty tells the other inmate.

"Yeah man. We need this before you get released. All our girlfriends are scared to death to bring the bag," the inmate adds.

He looks in the mirror, removing his durag in preparation for his visit. "This is hopefully one of my last runs, too. I'm on a violation. I can't afford another city bullet, bro. This gang shit just setting me back. My anxiety is on a million when I know she's on her way," Shorty tells him.

"Yo, I'll sign up for church later. If you need me to help you carry shit there, just come to my cell and we walk out together."

Shorty nods in agreement, gathering his clothes to jump in the shower. He is clearly anticipating the CO to call him for the visit. A fellow gang member walks by his cell and throws up a sign to him. He reciprocates.

Inside the Rikers Muslim Mosque, inmates gather and prepare for prayer. Deputy Amir, a slender Middle Eastern male in his early 40s, ex-convict turned volunteer civilian, with thick-lensed glasses begins service. About 22 inmates are in attendance of early morning service.

"As-salamu alaikum, brothers!" Deputy Amir shouts.

In unison all the inmates reply, "Wa-alaikum as-salam!"

"Unfortunately, Iman Aziz could not attend service today and has asked me to remind everyone that Ramadan is scheduled this coming Saturday after sunset. Please make sure you have signed up for meals to be delivered to you at your designated housing areas," he reminds the inmates as they sit in prayer position.

Inmate Dollar strolls in slowly from his work detail. He removes his footwear and dirty apron, "Brother Amir, as-salamu alaikum, my sincerest apologies. I could not get an escort officer before count time and…" Dollar explains.

Deputy Amir interrupts him, "Wa-alaikum as-salam, Mr. Parker, no worries. Find a spot," he sternly tells him.

He does exactly that and finds a space next to his friend and taps him to get his attention.

"That's a touchdown, you heard. Anyone tell you about the homie that they cut last night in dorm 12? That was

Shorty's boy. I'm not playing with these cats, bro," Dollar whispers to the inmate at the right of him.

"Shhh, we'll talk later man. This is not the right place or time," the inmate brushes him off quietly.

Dollar hates being ignored and gets up pushing guys out his way as he storms out of the mosque. He places his boots back on. Deputy Amir shakes his head in disbelief but continues prayer.

"Say he is Allah, the one and only great, for his children shall live forever," Deputy Amir continues service.

The correction officer supervising Jummah yells out to Dollar to stop running, but he pays him no mind. He continues ignoring everyone up the stairs in a fury. Dollar cuts the corner and slightly brushes shoulders with a leaned over Julissa.

"Parker, call someone. I feel really dizzy. Hurry!" Julissa fights to speak and tries to catch her breath. Exchanging one last glance at Dollar, she faints.

"What the fuck! Yo, CO! Help!" Dollar yells out.

There is nobody in the corridors during count time. He leans her against the wall and runs back to the mosque.

"Yo! Ms. Sanchez just fainted upstairs! Call the clinic man. She's sweating and pale, man!" he nervously explains.

The correction officer jumps up and rushes to her aide. He radios the control room about the medical emergency. Other corrections officers rush towards them.

"Get her some fucking water!"

Doctor Lau and another clinician exit the elevator and speed walk towards them to take her vitals. A few correction officers help place her on the gurney, guiding her towards the clinic, and close the door on Dollar's face.

"Parker! Where are you supposed to be? It's count time and you're in the corridor with no escort. Go back to the Mosque or to your housing area now!"

"I'm the one that found Sanchez! She'd be laying there helpless if I didn't run into her!" Dollar corrects.

The correction officer sighs and gives in, "Yeah, you're right. But I still need you somewhere until the count clears at least."

"You think she's going to be alright?" Dollar's voice is concerned.

He nods and pats him on the back.

"Sanchez. Hello, hello," Doctor Lau taps her. He places a damp rag dipped in rubbing alcohol under her nose. She slowly wakes up, disorientated. "You're in good hands. Don't worry."

"What's going on? What happened?" Julissa tries to get up.

"Seems like the heat got the best of you. You passed out from physical exhaustion it looks like."

Taking a sip of her bottled water she agrees.

"You need to go home and see your primary doctor as soon as possible. I suggest a physical and a review of your blood work prior to you returning to work, okay?" Doctor Lau suggested.

On the visitation floor Mya shares a laugh while holding her boyfriend's hands on the table separating them. Mya slowly pulls out a square-shaped item wrapped in duct tape from the bun of her hair and hands it over to Shorty when the officers are distracted. Shorty quickly places it inside his mouth with close precision.

"See how easy that was?" Shorty whispers.

"Yeah, whatever. Kiss me please."

They share a kiss. A female officer spots them and demands that they cut it out. The couple next to them get a head nod from Shorty. The couple pretends to argue and make a scene. The officer walks over to diffuse the problem. Shorty stops the officer in her tracks.

“Excuse me, Officer. I'm ready to leave the visit. She’s late for work.”

Surprised that he’s dismissing her before the visit hour is over, Mya is furious. She stands up quickly, “Fuck you, Shorty! I'm never pulling up here again, watch!” Mya shouts.

Shorty goes in for a hug over the table separating them. She walks out pissed. The officer on the floor signals the search officer in the room that he has an incoming inmate ready to go. He enters the partition to undress and get strip searched.

“You know the drill, footwear first then your jumper,” the search officer directs.

Throwing off his visit-issued slippers, he points at the camera, “I thought having that camera up there as I got undressed was a violation of my rights? That thing is looking directly at me,” Shorty questions

The officer turns and looks up. Shorty takes the contraband out of his mouth and grips it in his palm. Everything is going as planned.

“Yeah, man, whatever. Jumpsuit. Okay, get dressed. Hurry up,” the officer carelessly goes through the motions.

Shorty leaves.

Downstairs at the visitor registration area, Mya walks out teary-eyed towards the locker holding her phone. CO Jones notices her discomfort and bolts in her direction.

"Bad visit, huh?" Jones asks, already knowing what probably transpired.

"I hate coming here and seeing him sometimes," she vents.

"Yeah, I feel you. The commute does not make it any better either," he agrees.

She rolls her eyes.

Jones had gotten her number a few days ago when he noticed her frequently visiting. He attempted to take her out to eat one day. She declined, but it's obvious she does find him attractive. They text here and there.

"Don't remind me, I hate that, too."

"I mean, I'd gladly drop you off," he suggests.

Mya looks around. The female correction officers stare her down as she holds this conversation with Jones.

"Isn't that against the rules?" she questions.

"You had no problem doing something against the rules five minutes ago. What do you think, I'm blind? You think I don't know what you do every time you come up here?" he reminds her.

She's stuck and embarrassed.

“Listen, take the bus across the bridge and meet me at the diner on Astoria Boulevard. My lunch break is in about 20 minutes, but my boy is the area supervisor so he got me covered for the day,” CO Jones instructs her.

Mya smiles and her demeanor is calm, “You’re fucking crazy. But ok, I’m down.”

“No. What’s crazy is you risking your freedom bringing shit in here for a boy who doesn't give a fuck about you or himself. Go get on the bus and I’ll catch up to you.”

Right outside the building, Antonio looks through his cell phone waiting for the bus home. The visit route bus arrives next to the public transportation bus and Mya hopes off staring in his direction.

“Tony?! Is that you?” Mya screams.

“Oh shit! Mya? What are you doing over here?” his eyes widen with disbelief.

“My, uh, friend is locked up here. I just came to show love and drop off some clothes and money,” she lies.

“Oh okay, good for you. I just started working here. Well, technically…I'm doing on-the-job training, but I graduate soon. Actually, next Sunday,” he happily informs her.

She can't stop smiling. She's a lot younger than him, but she knows he's not wrapped up in any crime-driven activities, like most people from their neighborhood. In her mind, Antonio's like a breath of fresh air and full of positive vibes.

"That's so cool, Tony! I am so proud of you! Always knew you'd do something positive, unlike your brother."

Antonio shakes his head in agreement. They both get on the Q100 bus.

At the C-73 building, Warden Brown walks out on the phone and throws his duffle bag in the trunk of his departmental vehicle. He leaves to go check up on the co-worker he's always had a little thing for, Captain Mitchell. He looks through his contact list and calls her up. It rings.

"Crystal? This is Warden Brown. I am en route to the hospital to come see you. I hope you're hungry, my treat," he suggestively invites himself.

"Oh, no. Are you sure?" she questions embarrassedly.

"It's no trouble at all, trust me. And I'll be on the clock. I been needing to get out of this place. The fresh air will do me some good."

He gets into the car and exits the parking lot. At the same time, Correction Officer Jones tails right behind him.

Jones realizes his Warden is pulling up into the same diner he is expecting to meet Mya. He begins to panic. They both step out of their vehicles, parallel to one another. Jones knows he is not allowed to leave Rikers during his shift unless it has to do with the department.

"What the fuck man," Jones mumbles to himself, sweating profusely.

They exchange a fake smile. Jones knows he has some explaining to do. He tries to think of something quick, but the Warden will be able to smell the bullshit stench seeping through his pores. Before he can open his mouth with a reason for why is there, Warden Brown sparks the small talk.

"I remember being a meal runner when I first started in the department. You do know you're not supposed to leave the island on the clock unless it's a hospital run, right Officer Jones? But everyone does it, even me. This one's on me, but the next one is on you, young blood, so quit the habit before it gets you a command discipline," he states.

"I'm really sorry, sir. There won't be a next time," Jones apologetically replies.

"Go grab your food and return to post son."

Jones grabs his phone from his pants pocket to call Mya. He rather catch her later on than to be spotted out in public with an inmate's girlfriend while on the clock in full uniform after already being warned by his superior that this is unacceptable.

Mya and Antonio continue to converse about the job and career path he's about to start. She signals Antonio to hold his thought while she answers her cell phone.

"Hey!?"

"Hey, listen. I'm not going to be able to link with you right now. One of my supervisors just pulled up on me in the diner parking lot. Just go on without me. We can possibly link up later on, cool?" Jones tells her with embarrassment.

Mya stares blankly, glancing awkwardly at Antonio, "Well, can you meet me in Harlem?" she insinuates.

"Yeah. Yeah, cool. I'll call you around 7-7:30 when I leave the island."

He hangs up on her. She also puts her phone away.

"Sorry Tony. What were you saying?" she blushes.

"Nothing, really, I was just saying how I am happy for this opportunity. No more bagging groceries for minimum wage anymore, and now I can finally save up to move out of my mom's," he pauses, "On another note, aren't you supposed to be in school right now? Did you even graduate yet?"

"Well, not yet. This is my junior year though," Mya looks down timidly.

"Wow, you're still a little baby!" he jokes.

"No I'm not, shut up! I'm a grown 16, not a childish 16!"

"Wait…if you're not even 18, how did you visit your friend just now?" he interrogates.

Mya pulls out a fake ID from her back pocket, handing it over to him. She waits to catch his reaction. She's bold enough to carry it on her, but she fears judgment since she's known Antonio for basically her entire life, "There's always a way to do things, Tony."

He smirks at her clever bravery. They both smile. He's actually impressed more than anything. He dismisses her law-breaking. For him, she's just supporting a friend and is doing it by any means necessary. That equals loyalty and love in his book. Antonio deems those things priceless.

"Whatever you say, 'Jessica,'" he sarcastically replies, handing her back the fake ID.

Mya snatches it back from his hand in a playful manner and they talk the entire ride home.

Warden Brown purchases flowers at the gift shop in the hospital lobby. He wants to take this opportunity outside of work to express his interest in her, and make sure that she knows he is there for moral and emotional support, with secret hopes of eventually supporting her physically.

Sean and Leah walk in and rush to check in at the information desk behind Warden Brown. The information clerk is preoccupied with another visitor. Sean, panicking, pulls out his cell phone and calls her himself.

"Crystal! What floor and room are you!?"

Her heavily medicated voice picks up, "Room 340, Sean. Visits are 11-2 and 4-7 only so hurry upstairs."

Captain Mitchell hangs up as Warden Brown strolls into her room holding flowers, beating Sean to get to her first.

"You really shouldn't have, sir," she blushes through the pain meds.

Captain Mitchell has had her share of over using prescription medication, as well as mixing them with alcoholic beverages. Years back when she worked in Rose

M. Singer, the women holding facility on Rikers Island, she was savagely jumped in the recreation yard by four female inmates. The attack caused her to suffer a fractured jaw and multiple hairline fractures on her cheek bone. She was prescribed oxycodone and was out of work for nearly a year. She returned after a full recovery and was shortly after promoted to Captain. All the while, she was still purchasing pain medication even when she didn't really need them. That's how she met her boyfriend Sean, a local pill pusher from her neighborhood. They would get high together and they fell in love, whatever kind of love that could be.

"It's something light. How are you feeling?" he softly questions.

"Just a terrible headache and really sore, on top of my brand new car being totaled," she sighs.

"Well, that's replaceable. You made it out and that's all that really matters," Warden Brown comforts her, "Did you notify your immediate family members?"

"Yes, my fiancé and daughter are downstairs in the lobby now."

He stops grinning and stumbles. He wasn't expecting that answer. Everyone knew that she was a mother, but he swore she was single. Most of the rumors he's heard of her mentioned that she became a lesbian after giving birth and only sought romance with women, Officer Sanchez notably being one of her ex-partners.

"Fiancé?" his face screws.

"Well, Sean and I have been Domestic Partners for about 4 years now. It's documented because of his past situations so…"

Sean walks in mid-sentence holding their daughter's hand and some get well gifts.

"Hi mommy!" her daughter Leah shouts in a cute, squeaky voice.

He places Leah on the bed, ignoring Warden Brown on purpose. It's as if he's not even present in the room. Paying attention to her daughter, Captain Mitchell also neglects Warden. Feeling unwelcomed and uncomfortable, Brown slowly excuses himself.

"I'll let you enjoy your visit and speak to you later Capt. Please call if you need anything. There's a possibility the union representatives might stop by to check on your well-being," he reminds her as he makes his way out.

"Thank you so much for coming, Warden!"

"Not a problem, it's part of the job. Take care."

Sean pulls close the privacy curtain in his face before he even has a chance to respectfully step out, “Yeah, peace homie!” Sean says through the curtains.

Warden Brown shuts the door feeling defeated.

The sun starts to shine. The city is packed with traffic as everyone rushes to school or work. Antonio steps off the bus clutching his uniform shirt in hand, waving to Mya who remains on the bus for another stop. Walking towards his building, checking his texts, he’s approached by a neighbor.

“Tony! Say it ain't so bro! You look like those police academy recruit guys, man. Let me guess, can’t beat em, join em, huh?” the neighbor jokingly says while walking past him, cutting to the park in front of the housing projects.

“Yeah, man, this gig beats bagging groceries,” Antonio tells him taking pride in his decision to become a part of what many in his neighborhood believe to be the oppressor of occupations.

A group of men, ranging between the ages of 20-30, come out his building and are taken aback by Tony’s uniform. One of them spurts out, “Yo, CO, open my cell!”

and chuckling as he opens the door and enters the lobby and elevator.

Tony keeps his head high, passing the drug peddlers soliciting in the lobby; he hops on the urine filled elevator. Exiting, he hears the sound of loud music coming from his apartment, but more importantly, the smell of breakfast being made puts a smile on his face.

Antonio's younger sister Marisol, a chunky girl with Down syndrome who wears glasses and pigtails, rushes towards him for a hug as she welcomes him home.

"Tony! Hi!" Marisol greets.

"Hey, Mari, where's mommy?"

Marisol gestures with her fingers to her mouth, trying to communicate that she's in her room smoking. He places his uniform on the couch and walks to her room, knocking through the loud music. He's unable to get her attention and barges in without warning. His mother is in the middle of performing oral sex on a male companion.

"Hi mom."

Ana, startled, gets up to close the door in his face. She is a 39-year-old woman, who tries to maintain her youth as much as possible while battling a drug and alcohol addiction. She acts more like Antonio's sister than his mother since she conceived Antonio at the tender age of 18.

Even more surprisingly, she had his older half-brother Diego at 13, unable to get an abortion due to underlying complications with her thyroid disorder.

Ana walks out into the hallway, "Tony! You need to learn how to knock! What the fuck is wrong with you!" she furiously demands.

"I did ma! Who the fuck is that! Why the fuck is he in our house!" Antonio snaps back.

"That's my business, Tony! I'm never in your business! He's just an old friend anyway, relax!"

"And why are you smoking weed, especially while Marisol is here?" he questions her aggressively.

Ana looks behind Antonio and notices Marisol watching TV on the couch eating cereal. She peacefully is in her own little world.

"It's only weed, Tony. Be happy it's not the other shit like before, okay," she whispers.

Frustrated he goes and locks himself in his room. Ana's male friend steps out the door halfway and kisses her from behind. She kisses him back and runs to the fridge grabbing a juice box and quickly hands it to Marisol.

"Food's almost ready, Mari, okay?" she reminds her youngest.

Marisol innocently nods as she watches TV. Ana strolls back into the room and continues where they left off.

Antonio prepares for a quick shower. Looking through his cell phone, it rings in his hand. It's an incoming call from Diego.

"You have a collect call from an inmate at Greenhaven Correctional Facility. If you wish to accept this call, please press 1," the operator prompts him.

He presses 1 and puts the phone on speaker.

"My man! Where you been hiding? You haven't answered in months. What's up with you little bro?" Diego is excited on the other line.

"Never hiding big bro, I just been really busy. What's up? How are you holding up in there?"

Diego's coming closer to an almost 8 year prison sentence he is serving. He calls Antonio from time to time to check up on him, even randomly asking him for favors like three-way phone calls, care packages, and pictures. Prior to him being sentenced, Diego financially supported his entire family. Antonio never asked for a penny, but he did look up to his brother's lavish lifestyle.

"Aside from the politics that go on in here, I can't complain man. I'm just making the days count and not really counting the days, feel me?"

“I like that, man. Stay positive, bro. When are you coming home is the real question?” Antonio’s interest is slightly pretend.

“That's why I've been calling you, to give you the good news. I made my parole board so I’m on my way out in about 90 days, maybe less,” he is happy to deliver the good news.

Antonio’s eyes widen, “Well, guess who else has some good news? I graduate from the Correction Officers Academy next week!” he excitedly informs.

“Wait, you’re gonna be a pig like Julissa?”

Antonio is clearly offended and retorts aggressively, “I’m not a fucking pig, Diego! I took the test and passed it. They called me, and I'm about to graduate. It's a better opportunity for me than what I have now. Who else is gonna take care of mom and Marisol, huh?”

There are almost 10 seconds of awkward silence.

“Julissa is showing me the ropes. I trained with her last night matter of fact so…” Antonio continues.

“Calm down little bro. I'm just messing with you in all honesty. I'm proud of you, who am I to judge you?”

“Well, regardless man, I won't be picking up after this call. Even though you are family, it's a conflict of interest. Plus, you’ll be home soon so it’s pointless to notify the department about our communication," he pauses, "I gotta go. I love you and I'll see you once you touch down. Just let mommy know when you are back in town."

"I respect it, bro, just be careful. The Island is no joke. Make sure you let dudes know who's in charge," he reminds his little brother as he has his own idea of Rikers Island's etiquette.

They both hang up.

Diego grabs his ID from the State Correction Officer after leaving the phone booth, walking towards his friend lifting weights a few steps away from him. Diego has confusion written all over his face.

"What's good? Bad phone call?" he asks.

"Nah man, not at all. Probably the best phone call I've had since my whole bid started," Diego reassures.

The other inmate gets up, grabs his net bag, and they walk off to smoke.

Julissa's phone rings and she tries to answer through the shower curtain. Wet and annoyed, she puts the call on speaker. The jail operator recites an automated message and she rolls her eyes.

"You home right? How are you feeling?" Dollar's voice questions her.

Turning off the running water, she hops out to dry. "I'm better now, just lots of stress and physical exhaustion from doing so much overtime. I'm excused from work for two weeks and even when I do come back I'll be on light duty, so it's gonna be a while before I actually get to go back to my regular post or even be around your ass," she explains.

Dollar loudly sucks his teeth and shakes his head, "Wow! Aight! Word!"

"It's not my fault! Why are you catching an attitude?"

"Because, Ju, I have business to take care of in here and you're fucking up my flow, bitch!" he responds with rage.

She hangs up on him and throws her burner phone against the wall shattering the screen. They've maintained an on and off again relationship from the moment Julissa graduated the academy. One night after having a huge argument with her old boyfriend, Dollar was there to comfort her emotions. They bonded, and their frowned upon friendship grew. She'd always cook a meal for him and bring him new underwear, which quickly escalated after a few months. Since then, she's been able to make money from smuggling contraband to Dollar, one of the top Blood leaders on Rikers. Today she has realized that she's had enough. Not so much of the money she's acquired, but their relationship which has become solely business.

"I FUCKING HATE YOU!" she screams at the top of her lungs. She looks in the mirror teary eyed, angry with herself. Her luxury car, her penthouse apartment, none of it is worth her the emotional distress. She wants out.

CHAPTER 3

Shorty arrives back to housing from his visit. He bangs on the gate to get the attention of the correction officer in the bubble room, in a rush to return to his cell to unwrap and bag up the contraband he's received from Mya. This was mostly something he got into to satisfy his gang. He's the only one who is on Rikers as a result of a parole violation, but gang culture does not exempt you from carrying out the duties that strengthen the gang and give them an upper hand on the flow of drugs around the facility. He knows by falling in line with the structure, God forbid he were to end up coming back to Rikers, he'd stand in a better position.

"CO! 13! Cell back from the visit," Shorty shouts.

The door buzzes open and he walks right in. The CO on post is familiar with him and doesn't frisk him upon entering, something they were taught to exercise every chance they get when an inmate is returning to the housing area.

He speed walks down the gallery and the other inmates stare through the Plexiglas of their cells for their signal that everything went smoothly. Shorty is well known for what they refer to as "getting the bag." Many times, inmates get caught up because of another inmate throwing them under the bus.

Unbeknownst to Shorty, the security team is stationed outside the housing area. Security Captain Brian Davis, a 40-year-old with a shiny bald head and football player build, flashes his lights for the officer in the bubble room to quietly open the front entrance gate of the housing area. The officers sneak in. They run straight to Shorty's cell, startling the other inmates that are on the phone and in the dayroom watching TV. Shorty is like a deer in headlights when they catch him with the straight edged razors lined up on his bed and a few pieces of orange Suboxone strips, a very popular drug used to treat opiate addiction. It decreases withdrawal symptoms and it's known to give you the high of an opioid without the addictive trait like methadone.

"Open! 13!" Captain Davis announces right outside his cell.

The team rushes in, pinning Shorty to the ground and placing handcuffs behind his back while the officers recover the contraband laid on his bed and search for more.

"You really thought those cameras were inoperable, huh?" he questions Shorty.

Escorting him out, the other inmates watch the whole ordeal from inside their cells. After the team leaves with Shorty in handcuffs, rumors between the inmates begin that someone must have snitched him out. They snicker and whisper to one another on the tier.

Back at the visiting registration desk, the A-station bubble phone rings. Correction Officer Jones puts his cellphone back into his vest before answering.

"Visitation floor, Jones speaking."

It's Captain Davis on the other line, "Jones! What's going on player? Listen, inmate Christian Crespo. Do me a favor and check the name of his last visit. He left the floor and we caught him with some goodies."

Jones sits up properly from his seat and checks the computer log. He knew it was the girl he had been flirting with and planned to meet after his shift.

"Umm…Jessica Mercado, Capt.," he informs.

"If she ever comes back, restrain her from leaving. We got her little boyfriend and the razors she brings him," the Captain's voice is stern.

Jones shakes his head and takes in a deep breath. They hang up. He runs into the staff bathroom to call Mya.

Mya looks for her wallet while her sandwich is being prepared when her cell phone rings, and it's an unknown number this time.

"Hello? Who's this?"

"Yo! Listen to me, it's Jones. Can you still meet up later today? Like around six?" Jones whispers.

"Yeah, wasn't that the plan from the start?"

"Shit got crazy in here just now. Look, I'll be in my car on Broadway and 127th street around 6. Right under the 1 train station, ok?" he clarifies.

"Ok, sounds good, Mr. Jones," she jokingly calls him by his last name. She hangs up and grabs her food, shaking her head.

Captain Davis leaves his office and walks into the intake area to speak with the officers who have Shorty surrounded as he sits handcuffed in his underwear, shivering in the search room used for incoming inmates returning from court. Captain Davis steps right in front of him, kneeling at eye level, sizing him up and rolling up his crispy white uniform sleeves to his elbow. Each cuff that his sleeve goes up is more intimidating than the last.

"Would you like to put us on game?" Captain Davis questions in a passive tone.

“I got nothing to say! Suck my dick, bozo!” Shorty answers under his breath, never once looking the captain in the eye.

Captain Davis signals his fellow staff and one of them punches him from behind. Shorty falls flat on the ground, busting his nose and lip, dripping blood from both. The other CO guides him back to the chair. Shorty looks up at him and spits directly into his face. They rush him back to the ground with punches and kicks as he screams for them to stop. The blistering noise can be heard by the other inmates in the intake area placed in the outer cages, awaiting transport to court.

“Stop resisting!” two of the officers shout.

The inmates can't see, but they hear the ruckus occurring in the back room. They know from stories they've heard, or from their own past experiences, how the security team here gets down. The inmates yell at the top of their lungs, telling the correction officer staff to stop the obvious injustice. Shorty’s agonizingly screams while the others bang on the wall and shake their gates in protest.

Mya eats her sandwich in the park and smokes a blunt while she waits for Jones. He pulls up directly in front of her honking his horn. She inches her head in curiosity, then he rolls down his dark-tinted window. She timidly peeks inside and gets in.

"Hey, cute stuff! Where are we going?" she asks him, high as a kite.

He speeds off as soon as the light turns green, "Let's grab a drink at a bar, chill there for a bit," he recommends.

Mya nods her head no. Her fake ID might get declined, depending on the venue, and she doesn't want to risk the embarrassment. She's really interested in Jones. He's a prize in her eyes.

"Let's just chill here. Matter of fact, drive up to Riverside and 135th street under the highway," she suggests, "It's dark and really quiet all around there."

He nonchalantly agrees and drives.

"Ok, Officer Jones. Are you ever going to reveal your first name, or is it CO?"

"It's Jeffrey," he laughs.

Jones parks the car and they both unbuckle their seatbelts.

"But on the real, I got some fucked up news to tell you."

Mya's body language becomes stiff. She's caught off guard. He stares at her awkwardly.

"What? Tell me!" she's nervous.

"Homeboy you came to visit today was caught about an hour after you left and is probably facing charges. He got caught red-handed and on camera. He's getting sent to the box! Captain Davis drools over contraband-related incidents, so he's going to make sure he hits him as hard as possible, figuratively and…physically," Jones feels bad to have to deliver this news.

Mya is relieved by the news, "Oh, man, you had me thinking it was a life or death situation," she calmly tells him after.

"Wait, that doesn't bother you at all? Isn't that your boyfriend?" he questions.

She pulls out a pack of cigarettes, offering him one, "Man! Fuck that! He uses me anyway! We fuck here and there when he's home, but I'm tired of his shit! I'm tired of the back and forth, I'm tired of these little kid games. I'm too grown for all of this. It's annoying, it's time-consuming. I'm done."

Jones is stunned by it all, "Well, I figured since you risk your freedom for the guy and.."

She cuts him off, deviating from the whole topic, "I can smoke in the car, right?"

He nods yes, handing her his lighter. Oddly enough, he is turned on by her sassiness and attitude towards this guy.

It's nighttime. Antonio slowly wakes up to a glare coming from a creak in his door.

"Tony! Come eat!" Marisol whispers.

"Okay, Mari, I'm coming."

Rubbing the sleep from his eyes, he steps into the dining room. He notices his mother serving food as her male friend from earlier sets up plates and utensils.

"Tony, Roberto's joining us so don't eat all the flan I baked. You're going to have to share, okay?"

Marisol playfully places a bib on Roberto and then one on Antonio. They both smile at her innocence.

"Your mom tells me you're graduating from the Police Academy soon, Tony. That's a good career, man. Congrats," Roberto's attempt at small talk is weak.

"Corrections, not police officer," Antonio corrects him.

"Tony, how's Julissa? Has she been informative and all that with you?" his mom asks.

"Yeah, little by little. Damn, that reminds me! I forgot all about her incident today, I'll be back," he gets up from the table leaving his plate barely touched.

He hates the energy from his mother's boyfriend. He can't wait to save up enough money and move out, even though he would hate to leave his little sister alone. He goes back to his room to grab his phone and dials Julissa's number.

"I have a feeling he doesn't want me to be here, Ana," Roberto says.

"Don't take it personal, babe. He's a nice kid, trust me."

Julissa smokes a cigarette as she pours herself some red wine. Her other phone rings disturbing her tranquility.

"Can I get ten minutes of fucking peace! Damn!" she shouts out loud to herself.

It's Antonio calling. She turns down her music and puts the glass down, pressing accept on her phone.

"Hi, Tony. What's up?"

"Hey, I know you won't be coming in tonight after your whole fainting episode."

"Yup! That's a negative, sir! I'm going to milk this for as long as I can. I need a good break from that fucking hellhole," she smiles.

"I feel you. I guess I'll be taking the bus tonight," he says, defeated at the thought of doing so.

"What I can do for you is call central control and ask for a favor, get you the same post from last night. You do remember everything that needs to be done, right? You're smart. You got this, Tony," she affirms.

"Yeah, I remember. That would be great! Listen, get well and I hope to see you soon, Ju!"

They hang up and she puts her phone on Do Not Disturb, pouring herself more wine and turning on the music. She goes through her drawer and pulls out a vibrator. She lays back and goes to town.

It's bright and early the next morning. The corrections union president, Neil Simmons, a 50-year-old African American male with a political presence who is always sporting a huge grin, has been with the department for over 30 years. He's fought for the rights of correction officers, helped make the jail safer, implemented the right to carry pepper spray, rallied to get stab-proof vests, and got legal representation to all who needed it. He's loved by many, but hated by few. Some call him an "officer's officer."

He takes a sip of his coffee as he is being chauffeured by his vice president, Doug Frazier, mid 40s and heavyset guy known as a yes-man, across the Rikers Island Bridge. Their department vehicle is heavily tinted.

"Are you ready for another term?" Frazier asks after he turns down the jazz music. He quickly sips his coffee.

"I'm always ready, Doug! Why do you think I show my face here as often as I do?"

"To prove you're for the people?" Frazier is unsure.

"Exactly! And to hand out these correction officer union water bottles to all my beautiful thirsty female COs. You never know who might want to sip," Simmons jokes.

He grabs a water bottle from the backseat, laughing as Frazier slows down and rolls down the window gazing at a passing female officer exiting her car. He waves for her to come.

"Here you go beautiful. It's gonna be almost a hundred degrees by noon they said," Frazier flirts.

They hand her two bottles.

"Don't forget to vote next month, sis! Every vote counts! Have a safe tour, okay?"

When she walks away, they spill out the word "DAMNNN" in unison. They both stare at her voluptuously curvy body as she gets into the employees' route bus that takes most of the correction staff to their designated buildings. Those who are allowed to drive straight in are Captains, Assistant Deputy Wardens, and Wardens. Some staff may have the luxury of driving straight in, depending on their assigned post. The union president has his own parking spot just for himself and the staff on his board.

"Doug, I love this fucking job."

They pass the emergency service trailer, where the ESU officers are on standby for alarms or incidents that may get out of hand. They're ready at all times to deal with riots, hostage situations, fires, flooding, and so on. Inside, emergency service correction officers enjoy their breakfast. Their Captain is interrupted just before taking a bite of his bagel. The department radio and alarm go off, asking them for further assistance inside the punitive segregation box at the OBCC building.

"We have a hostage situation involving an officer in the box. Suit up. Let's Go!" shouts ESU Captain Adams.

They all drop their food and rush towards the awaiting truck. Only about a 2-minute drive towards the building, an unconscious correction officer is seen handcuffed to a delirious and obviously disturbed inmate, Jackson, who has barricaded himself inside the shower and is demanding to be taken out of the box. He paces back and forth, dragging the officer like a ragdoll.

"Call the psych! Ms. Perry!" Jackson screams from inside the shower.

Assistant Deputy Warden Saunders, a young faced Caucasian female with piercing blue eyes tries to calm him down through the open slot in the door that stands between them. Multiple correction officers suit up in riot gear surrounding the area.

"Mr. Jackson, calm down, okay? We need you to please release the officer before someone gets seriously hurt! Ms. Perry, the Psych is on her way! Okay?" she states and keeps composure.

"Shut the fuck up! Call Perry! Now!" he continues to yell.

Psychologist Ms. Perry, a late 50-year-old Caribbean woman with thick glasses and a calming demeanor walks towards the corridor, escorted by an officer and the ESU Captain. There are many variables to dealing with the mental health population here at Rikers. Certain precautions need to be exhausted before things get physical, not to mention that these inmates share a particular strength when under certain medications, on top of their unpredictability. Only in these instances does the mental health clinician and psych have a certain authority to give direct orders to the officers. They're the trained professionals, most officers have not been educated enough to realize when an inmate is under a psychosis or going through a mental breakdown. A study has stated that significantly 77% of the seriously injured inmates had received a mental illness diagnosis during their incarceration, especially those in restrictive housing units, who for the most part are placed there due to their violent acts towards staff and other inmates.

"Ms. Perry! Thank God! Inmate Tyler Jackson, cell 31, is having an extremely violent episode. In the process of being escorted to his routine shower, he punched my officer, handcuffed himself to him, and is blaming it on his medication. Either you get him to comply and surrender or we go in using the electric stun shield to subdue him and proceed with force," Saunders explains.

Ms. Perry takes a quick peek through the shower slot door locking eyes with Jackson. He stops in motion and slowly makes his way closer to the door slot. Ms. Perry looks out towards the officers behind her. She inhales deeply.

"I'm going to try my best."

They all nod in agreement.

"Mr. Jackson, hi honey. It's Ms. Perry. Can you please remove the cuffs from yourself and from the correction officer? Surrender to them peacefully so I can assess the problem you are having with your medication. We can speak one on one with no interruptions in the office once this whole ordeal is over. I can even get you a phone call to call your grandma. How does that sound?" she pleads through the door, pressing her face against the dirty, peeling paint.

"Ms. Perry! They mess with my life. They are not feeding me right! And they're messing with my medication! They won't turn my lights off! I haven't showered in over 6 days! Can you please get me out of here, Ms. Perry! Please!" he begs.

She looks behind her, signaling the extraction emergency service officers to give her one more minute. "I will put in the proper paperwork along with a review of your medication, just please remove the handcuffs from the officer right now. We cannot move forward if you have him inside there with you. He might have a severe concussion and need medical attention just like you will need once you release him," she continues to explain and slowly backs away, giving enough room for the officers to charge in.

In any other instance, she'd tell them to stand down, but there's an officer still in there with him and she knows how violent Jackson can be. She’s been dealing with him since his days as an adolescent in C-74, the youth offender building on Rikers which houses young men ages 16-18 years old.

The team buzzes open the sliding door, charging at inmate Jackson the second they see him unlocking the handcuffs. They push Ms. Perry out of harm's way, disbursing chemical agents; they drag out the still unresponsive officer and attempt to detain a crying and screaming Jackson. Other inmates caged in the box unit cause noise and more ruckuses, banging from inside of their cells in an attempt to cheer on his behavior.

“You’re breaking my arm! CO!” Jackson cries at the top of his lungs.

“Stop resisting, Jackson! Stop resisting!” Ms. Perry yells as officer escorts her down the stairs and into the A-station bubble.

CHAPTER 4

It's the Correction Officer Ceremonial Graduation Day. Officers take pictures with their families as the room filled with newly appointed correction officers and other promoted staff celebrate. Antonio's arm is tugged by his little sister Marisol who pulls him down for hugs and kisses.

"Congrats, Tony! You did it!" Marisol shouts.

He hands his mother his cellphone so she can take a picture of them.

"I'm truly proud of you, Tony. You deserve this after all the hard work you've put in. I know in my heart you'll be great," Ana expresses with watery eyes.

After they hug, a joyful Julissa creeps behind them both.

"Hi, Titi! Hi, Mari! Hello, Mr. CO!" Julissa greets.

"Juli! Hi, my love. I'm so happy you made it! How are you feeling?" Ana hugs and embraces her niece.

"I'm ok, Titi. I couldn't miss this for the world. My little cousin Tony is following in my footsteps," she teases.

They all share a laugh as they watch the Union President from afar greeting and congratulating every one of the rookie officers present. He takes pictures and gives quick formal advice to those who have questions or concerns starting their journey as New York City's boldest.

"Excuse us, Titi. Tony, let me introduce you to our union boss. He's really cool and a great person to know if you ever find yourself in a jam. Come on!" she grabs his hand, walking to Simmons.

"Wait. You guys are friends like that?" he asks.

"I'm friends with everyone, Tony. Why do you think any favor that I need I get? I'm practically untouchable in this department."

Simmons looks up and sees them approaching from his peripheral, "Is that who I think it is?"

She leans in and receives a juicy kiss from him on her forehead. They've had their share of fun. Not too long ago Simmons paid for a vacation for her and another co-worker, and she paid him back in other ways.

"Hi, Neil! How are you? How's the wife?" she flirts.

He extends his hand towards Antonio before responding to her semi-unwanted question.
"I'm blessed like always, beautiful. Is this your husband?" Simmons questions.

Nervously shaking his hand back, Antonio nods in disagreement. He remains quiet and guarded.

"No sir, we're just family," he speaks with shyness.

"Antonio this is your…excuse me, our union president Mr. Neil Simmons. He's great, anything you need he'll work hard to get for us, which is why I am hoping he gets re-elected, too."

"Nice to meet you, Antonio, and just like your..."

"Cousin..." Julissa continues for him.

"Cousin, Juli, said, I'm here for if you need. Take my card. It has my personal cellphone number as well as some other contact info. Give me a call for anything ranging from advice to Knicks game tickets to an attorney. No worries. Just tell me," he pulls a card out of his wallet and places it in Antonio's hand the way grandparents do when sneaking money to their grandchildren.

Trying to resist smiling, Antonio nods and glances over to a fellow female graduating classmate he's been eyeing for months. They gained a small friendship over the four months of the academy. Antonio would always flirt, but respectfully because he knew she had a boyfriend.

"Thank you, sir, I really appreciate it!" he brings his focus back to Neil.

Antonio excuses himself from the conversation and bee-lines towards newly appointed classmate CO Tiffany Thompson, a fresh faced, well-rounded young woman who carries herself with class and respect. He hopes to congratulate her and possibly start some small talk. She notices him and smiles, waving her hand. She gestures for him to come over to her.

"Tony! Finally, right? Longest four months ever!" Tiffany expresses taking off her graduation hat.

"Yes! I know! Are you scheduled to work tonight? They don't have me on until Sunday and I'm working the midnight shift," he asks.

"I work tomorrow, but I'm starting off the 3-11 shift."

"Ok, ok not bad," he nervously answers.

There's a moment of awkward silence between them. He wants to ask her to dinner, but can't come to it.

"I gotta go, Tiff. Going out to eat with the family, but text me, cool?

She nods in agreement.

Before he departs, they get interrupted by another graduating classmate. Rakim Mohammad, a dark-skinned, bald-headed, obnoxious, but extremely friendly, guy greets Antonio with a brotherly hug and extends his right hand to Tiffany with all smiles. His teeth are so white, it's as if they glow in the dark.

"We did it, guys! Let's celebrate!" Mohammad shouts, causing those around him to turn back.

They both give each other a still look of embarrassment.

"I'm about to go to my favorite restaurant with the family, man. Maybe in a few weeks after everyone settles would work better for me. How about you, Tiff?"

"Yes, definitely," Tiffany blushes.

She gets called by her parents for a picture and dismisses herself in a respectful manner, leaving them to converse. Mohammad, who is overly excited with emotions, looks at Antonio and his eyes widen more.

"Hey, man, that's all you. You better jump on that before the football player looking officers come for her. Remember our first job training night? After the alarm?" Mohammad reminds him.

Antonio laughs, "We're just cool, man. She was with me during the physical training and deadly physical training at the range. We had lunch together, but I think she has a boyfriend already, and I believe he's on the job, too."

"Damn...well, there are enough chicks on the Island for us to shop around once we get in there and establish a cool reputation," Mohammad jokes.

"If that's your main objective, you're going to burn yourself out brother."

They both chuckle. Mohammad suggests they exchange phone numbers and social media handles before they leave.

Antonio is filled with good energy and positivity for his new venture. He's not a civilian anymore and he sees longevity in being a correction officer. He notices the newly appointed captains and wardens around him and he knows within due time he's going to rise through the ranks. Going to college for Criminal Justice wasn't in the plan, but he plans on taking full advantage.

The sun settles over the beautiful New York City skyline. The family continues the celebration and grabs a table at their favorite family diner. Antonio, Marisol, Ana, and Julissa enjoy the rest of the night. Antonio's mother walks out to pick up an incoming phone call. Scooting to his left, Julissa taps him.

"Your mom looks really good, Tony."

"Yeah she does. She's laid off the hard stuff for over 6 months now. I'm proud of her."

Ana comes back to the table with a surprise that no one expected. Antonio's older half-brother walks slowly behind her, timidly holding a gift bag and kissing Julissa and Marisol from behind. Antonio's jaw drops in confusion and amazement. He hasn't seen his older brother in years, a few phone calls here and there, but never once did he go to visit him. It's always been a love/hate relationship with them. When he left, Antonio had to pick up all of the responsibility Diego left behind because Antonio's dad went away to prison at a young age then got deported after he was released.

"Surprise!" Ana shouts.

"Diego? We just spoke a few days ago. You told me it was soon, but I didn't expect it to be this soon," Antonio's confusion slightly surpasses his excitement.

"It was all premeditated, little bro. Mom and I would talk to each other all the time while I was gone, she invited me here tonight so we can all celebrate."

He takes a seat and plays with Marisol while they all embrace him. The only one not as enthusiastic is Julissa. They've had an awkward relationship since Diego ended up in Rikers on his last charge. Diego expected his cousin to look out for him. He heard through the grapevine that she would bring drugs in for certain guys and he even knew about her sexual relationships with two inmates. He pulled her to the side one day when they crossed paths and she got him kicked out of the building for even bringing up the subject.

"So, Diego, did you learn your lesson, or this is just a part of the game?" she belittles him.

"Be nice, Juju. People make mistakes, we all do. I'm not perfect, you're not perfect, Tony's the most angelic one out of all the adults at this table and he's not perfect. Let's move forward and celebrate a new chapter, in peace," Ana interjects.

Julissa agrees. Diego waves to the waiter and whispers to him to bring a bottle of wine as he hands over a gift bag to his brother. He wants to show his appreciation and growth throughout the time he has been gone. After all, Antonio has taken care of the house, their mom, their younger sister, and continuously worked towards his goals, never getting sidetracked. Diego admires his ambition.

"What's this, man? You just got out, where did you get money to buy anything?" Antonio jokes.

"Just open the box, bro!" Diego laughs anxiously.

Antonio does exactly that. He pulls out what looks like a small jewelry box, and takes off the top. He reveals the car keys to everyone at the table in confusion.

"Car keys? What?"

"My old car, Tony, it's yours. It's clean, low miles, all the paperwork is up to date, still insured and paid off, it's yours, bro."

Julissa and Ana both look at one another in awe.

"I heard you were still taking the bus, and now going into work I figured you'd need it more than me. Parole won't allow me to drive for another 6 months anyway, probably after my drug treatment and anger management programs are completed," he explains.

Antonio can't believe it. Today has really been a great day for him.

"Wow, man, this is surreal. I was actually saving everything I made to buy a car, but thank you! I owe you, man, for real."

Julissa side eyes Diego. Ana becomes emotional and grabs her sons' hands and asks everyone to get into a small prayer. They bow their heads.

"God, thank you for reuniting my family here tonight in celebration for everyone moving forward in life. Please give us strength and protect us from our vices and evil. Amen."

Everyone at the table responds in unison, "AMEN!"

The very next day on Rikers Island, the roll call breaks and the correction officers slowly make their way to their assigned posts as they bicker and small talk with one another. Rookie correction officer Mohammed steps off to the side and fixes his utility belt, a female captain joins him and stands aside him.

"This is your first night alone, correct?" she questions.

"Yes ma'am," he responds.

"5 main is a high classification housing area. Those inmates can run circles around you so be mindful. These are gentlemen that have been on Rikers for years," she continues.

He leans in and listens closely to her every word.

"And I know for a fact you're going to be stuck in overtime for the 7-3 shift. There's a lot of call outs today into tomorrow since it's Memorial Day weekend. Take advantage of the fact that they are locked in, but once you lock out your workers to serve breakfast, be cognizant of your surroundings."

"Yes ma'am, thank you," Mohammad becomes uneasy.

She walks away as he makes his way towards the housing area. He arrives at the gate and yells "5 Main!"

The officer in the bubble, CO Dawson, a small framed, but physically fit, older man turns down his loud radio and looks back, happy to see the officer relieving him from his post and it's early. He grabs the keys and comes to open the gate.

"My man! You're early and that's a blessing. Working 3-11 in 5 main is no joke and they locked the house down. There was a 2 on 1 fight at approximately at 8pm so they've been locked in since then. It's Memorial Day weekend so once I cross that bridge, I am going straight to the bar!" Dawson speaks with great joy.

"They had a fight? Was anyone hurt?" Mohammad is concerned.

"The one guy they jumped got it pretty bad. I didn't really get to see it because I was in the bathroom, but I have an inmate who cleans up for me. I call him 'Mr. Info' cause he keeps me in tune with the politics of the house. You know, who's in what gang, who's bringing in the drugs, who's got beef, and who owes money, etc.," Dawson explains as if it's a regular occurrence.

He shakes his head trying to take all this in as Dawson walks him to the bubble. He shows him the keys, shows him that all the razors are back, shows him where the toilet paper, toothbrushes, toothpaste and soaps are, in case the inmates ask him for it, along with the incident reports he had to write due to the fight that transpired on his shift.

"Now, remember, you're all alone till 7am when your other officer arrives. She's going to take your position here in the A-station bubble and you're going to be on the floor with the inmates. Pretty sure you're going to be stuck doing overtime and pretty sure it's going to be here so make sure you do your 30 minute rounds and have it all together, copy?"

"Copy," Mohammad takes in all the steps.

Mohammed grabs the keys and does his physical count, looking into the cells of every inmate in his housing area, making sure they are still alive and breathing. He looks through the Plexiglas and sees many inmates munching on snacks, others listening to their radio, others reading or praying. Once he finishes, he signs his count slip and gives it to Dawson assuring his count is clear and correct.

"62 inmates?"

"Correct! And on the first try? That's impressive, young blood!" Dawson congratulates him.

Mohammed smiles, feeling accomplished.

"Remember they're quiet and calm now, but not for one second should you sleep on these guys. They're listening and watching every move you just made, and trust me they heard our whole conversation. They're putting on a front right now. Keep your head up and your eyes open, and the most important thing right now is to LET ME OUT!" he bursts into laughter.

They walk out the bubble and he opens the gate for Dawson, "Alright, brother, get home safe!"

Trying to gather all the information and knowledge he just received, Mohammed sits in the A-station and signs himself into the log books and recounts the razors. He hears one inmate from the A-side of the house yell to the B-side of the house. An inmate yells at the top of his lungs.

"Whoopty!" a call to his fellow Bloods.

The other inmates reply back, "Whoopty!"

"Yo, we got a new k-9 for the night you heard! Put that in the air!" the inmate continues to yell.

Mohammed is unaware of what these things exactly mean. He starts to write down the words that are unfamiliar to him. Out of nowhere, all the inmates in the housing area start to bang on their cell doors and start screaming at one another. The noise can be heard from corridors away.

Mohammed starts to panic and flashes the lights in the house in hopes they stop and calm themselves down.

After 2 minutes of what seems to be an eternity, he yells from the top of his lungs, “Fellas! On! The! Noise!”

The banging slows down, but not entirely.

Mohammed grabs the keys and walks onto the A-side clutching his flashlight in one hand and keys in the other. After passing multiple cell doors to see who initiated the ruckus, he feels a warm splash of water hit the whole left side of his face and upper body. Mohammed is stunned in his tracks and wipes his eye, crouching over, taking a pause to register what just happened. He can't believe what just happened. The inmates burst out into laughter and commence with the banging on the cells and loud noises, only getting louder. Mohammed's mouth opens slightly and a drop of the liquid he has been hit with enters his mouth, he smells and tastes urine.

“I’m going to fucking kill you!” he furiously screams.

He sprints to the bathroom and washes his face with massive amounts of soap and water. He’s so furious, he begins to shake in embarrassment and shame. Going back and forth with himself, he resorts to pulling the emergency pin on his utility belt, right alongside his pepper spray.

“What the fuck man! Why me!” he says to himself.

The pin is pressed and the housing area A-station phone rings. He dries himself with brown paper towels and opens the door answering the call.

“Officer Mohammad, 5 main,” he answers.

“Officer, what's going on in your house? Did you press your pin by accident? Do you need assistance? Is this an accidental discharge?” it’s the same captain who warned him previously from inside the control room.

“I was just sprayed with urine while checking in on the inmates. I was splashed through the cell door,” he explains with embarrassment.

“Do you know what cell it came from directly? There's a team on their way, open your house gate and direct them to the cell accounted for doing so,” she tells him.

“Yes, ma’am,” he answers defeated.

He walks over to the gate with his keys, as the inmates still continue to make noise. Peeking his head out, he sees the alarm lights in the corridor are flashing indicating that the alarm is still in progress. Even though it’s the midnight shift, there’s always a response team at hand to defuse any fight, suicide attempt, or medical emergency, regardless of the inmates being locked in for the night.

The captain and officers suited up in riot gear enter the housing area. One of the suited officers takes off his helmet, “What side?”

“A-side, 11 cell!” he points.

They walk to the cell and can visibly see urine stains on the side of that cell door,
“Buzz open 11 cell!”

Mohammed buzzes the cell door open and the first officer in the response team enters the cell as the other officers stand by. The inmate responsible steps out in plastic flex cuffs dressed in only a white shirt and basketball shorts, sporting house slippers. He’s escorted with no further incident. Passing the A-station bubble, the inmate and Mohammed lock eyes for the first time.

“Give me his floor card. Make sure you write an incident report and an infraction report. I will come to pick it up from you in the morning. Once one of my officers takes suits down, they will come and relieve you to go to the clinic to get cleared by medical,” the Captain orders.

“Yes, ma'am.”

Mohammed walks out behind them and locks the gate. The house is so quiet you could hear a pen drop.

Looking for the paperwork he was asked to fill out by his captain, he shed a tear and looked up at the housing area illuminated by a few exit door lights. He's in anguish. His first night as correction officer was in no way what he had planned.

CHAPTER 5

The bar is filled to capacity with people enjoying themselves and Rikers staff unwinding. Officer Dawson is on his 7th beer, scrolling through his phone and not really chatting with anyone. He reaches for his car keys and slowly makes his way to the men's bathroom. Upon entering, he stumbles. He washes off his face in an attempt to relieve his inebriated self. He exits and walks to his vehicle, parked directly in front of the establishment. His vision blurs, but mentally, he feels sober enough to drive home which is only 15 minutes away at this hour. There's no traffic, he reminds himself. He takes the local streets in an attempt to be more cautious, making sure he obeys every stop sign and light. His mission is complete. Parking the car at the corner of his residence, he makes his way into his building.

Scrambling for his key and slowly making his way up the flight of stairs, he can hear a woman's voice pleading and screaming for help. He bursts through his apartment door and looks around before realizing that the noise is coming from the bathroom next to his daughter Kayla's room.

"Kayla!!" he shouts frantically.

Dawson finds his daughter being viciously assaulted by her boyfriend. This isn't the first time. Dawson has kicked him out and prevented him from entering his house before, once he found out about his violent behavior. In a drunken rage, Dawson attacks him and they wrestle into the sink. Kayla runs out to the living room, bloody faced and bruised up, crying and screaming hysterically.

"Get the fuck off me, man!" her boyfriend screams.

"I told you to never set foot in here you fucking clown! Now I'm going to teach your ass something," Dawson reminds him.

"Let me go! Get your foot off my neck, man! Kayla!" he struggles to get Dawson off.

They continue to fight as Kayla's boyfriend chokes Dawson with his left hand. Gripping his throat with his right hand and reaching for his personal protection firearm, Dawson unclips it and they both have a grasp of the weapon. Dawson gains momentum, steps away, and gets control.

"Kayla!" he yells out.

TWO GUNSHOTS.

Kayla runs in screaming, "NOOOOOOOOOOOO!"

"He tried to shoot me first! Kayla!"

She is crying and stunned at what has transpired.

Her boyfriend lays lifeless in a pool of blood with two gunshot wounds directly to his chest inches from each other. The horrific scene causes Dawson to get up and throw up into the toilet. He sobers up and gathers himself mentally. Kayla is lost for words and in complete shock.

"Call 911! Kayla! Call 911! Tell them he reached for my firearm and that I am a member of service. I'm a correction officer! Go!"

She grabs her cell phone from her back pocket, still holding her boyfriend's hand in hopes he can be revived once the paramedics arrive. Her dad walks over to the living room in a complete daze. With the sound of the gunshots at such a close proximity, his ears are still ringing. He kneels and prays.

About a 15-minute drive away, Jones and Mya passionately kiss from the shower onto his king-sized bed. His spacious and well-decorated room is lit with candles as R&B music plays in the background.

After climaxing, they both lay next to each other gasping for air.

"Wow," she says catching her breath.

"I know. Damn, that was good," he looks at her inhaling deeply.

"It was, but the wow was more so because you came inside me. You only wore a condom for the first round before the shower and you just came inside me."

"We should be good. You want to roll up? I'm off for the next three weeks, I can afford to smoke."

Mya sits upright on the bed and grabs the marijuana out of her purse on the dresser. "Here," she hands him a pre-rolled joint.

She's obviously bothered at how careless he seems. It triggers her and puts her in a mood.

"Can I be honest with you about something?" she asks him.

"Yeah, what's up?" he replies coughing and heaving heavy. He's not used to the smoke inhalation. He scrolls through his social media feed not really paying her demeanor any mind.

"How old are you again?" the question comes out of Mya's mouth slowly.

"33...why? How old do you think I am?" he sternly questions her.

"Well, that was my next question to you. How old do *you* think *I* am?"

"What? What are you trying to say? You're making me nervous."

Mya takes a deep breath, gets off the bed, and gathers her bra and panties from the floor. She sighs.

"I'm only 15 years old...and"

He cuts her off, "Wait! Wait wait wait wait, hold up, what? 15! You playing some sick ass game or something? Stop playing with me, Jessica!"

Mya, visibly nervous and concerned, tries to get fully dressed in the midst of the back and forth. She pleads.

"Don't be mad, okay. I can explain. My name's not Jessica either. I've used a fake ID when I go to visit Shorty."

Jones is in complete disbelief and confusion, anger is building.

"Who the fuck are you then? Tell me the truth about everything! Everything!" he demands.

Her eyes begin to water and she begins to sob slowly, gathering her words,

"My real name is Mya. I'm 15 and I turn 16 in four months. I dropped out of high school and I help Shorty, my boyfriend, sell his weed while he's gone. I bring him drugs and razors whenever I go to visit," she explains.

She can feel the tension rising and she backs away close to the door, in case he attempts to lash out at her. He shakes his head.

"Wow, are you fucking serious!? Where are you going? I'm not going to hurt you, man, relax!"

"I'm really sorry. I just didn't know how to be honest with you. Ever since you got my number weeks ago, we would text constantly and I got lost in our conversation. I meant no harm. Just know I really like you. Yes, I have a boyfriend, but it's obvious he's not that important to me," she continues.

"So, now what? I can't be with you. It's illegal, for one. For two , I'm an officer which makes it worse, and for three, this is basically rape, whether you consent or not you don't have any consent in this state or in this country for that matter. I'm twice your age, Mya! What the fuck!"

She shrugs helplessly. She can't find a way to respond to him and sobs even more, dropping her clothes and sitting by the door.

"I just really hope I'm not pregnant," she whispers, loud enough for him to hear.

Jones gets up from the bed and quickly grabs her belongings, grabs her by the neck, and escorts her out the apartment.

"Get the fuck out my house you lying ass bitch!"

Mya falls to the floor as he throws her bags and clothes on top of her, slamming the door. She crouches over and cries hysterically. She eases up and walks towards the elevator half naked.

The following morning, Ms. Perry types a progress report on her desktop about the inmates on her caseload. She hears the alarm go off once again. It's been going off every 20 minutes since she arrived, and the screams and bangs from the inmates in the Box down the hall from her office have not allowed her to focus. She's so stressed out, she begins to cry. The noise becomes unbearable, and she closes and locks her door. Ms. Perry opted out of working at a hospital to work on Rikers Island; the hazard pay was what lured her in. Her phone rings.

"Good morning. Mental health, Ms. Perry."

Warden Saunders is on the other line, "Ms. Perry, that last alarm is in response to Inmate Jackson again. I have a rookie female officer who pushed the alarm. During her rounds, she noticed him attempting to tie a noose around the light fixture. Can you please come to the Punitive Segregation Unit, cell 30?"

Ms. Perry takes a deep breath in, exhales slowly, and wipes the tears from her eyes, "I'm on my way, Warden."

She exits her office and walks toward the housing area. The officer in the A-station bubble buzzes the gate for Ms. Perry. A group of correction officers surround Jackson's cell. CO Tiffany's first day on the job has started off in the wrong direction.

"Warden, is that the mental health clinician?" Tiffany questions.

Warden Saunders looks behind her and waves Ms. Perry in.

"What's going on with Jackson? He's trying to get out of this unit, too?" Ms. Perry asks while shaking her head.

"Hello, Ms. Perry. It's my first day and I went to do my routine rounds and 30 cell was reading his book the first few times, but out of nowhere he starts banging on the cell door and I run towards him to see what's happening. It's like he called me to watch him hang," she speeds through what happened.

"Slow down, slow down, so he called you to watch him?" she questions, confused.

"Yes!"

Ms. Perry walks to Inmate Jackson's cell. Jackson sees her approaching through a small crack. He hides the noose by the toilet.

“Ms. Perrrrryyyyyyy!” Jackson sings her name in a melody tone.

“Why are you acting out, Jackson? I moved you from the Box and got the Warden to give you your radio and books and a blanket you shouldn't even have considering your mental health level,” she explains.

The inmates on Rikers are given mental health levels for housing and custody purposes. The care level includes inmates with stable mental health conditions requiring chronic care appointments and individual psychology health services that can occur every few days depending on the severity.

“I was just playing with her, Ms. Perry. She's brand new. I'm just trying to break her in. Anyways, how many more days do I have to do before they release me back to population?” he jokingly asks.

Tiffany and Warden Saunders slowly walk over to his cell.

“Jackson, why are you continuously messing with my staff? Ms. Perry has done everything in her power to get you out the Box. You only have 2 days left in here. They passed a new law, as of Monday, no adolescents in the Box. Be patient,” Saunders lets him know.

He smiles and sits on his bed, relieved.

"Warden Saunders, where's the S.P.A?" Tiffany questions her superior.

"Excuse me?" Saunders replies offended.

"The suicide prevention aide? The inmate assigned to watch the other inmates in case they try to commit suicide while..."

She cuts her off, sternly, "I know what an S.P.A. is, officer. I didn't get appointed the position I have by not knowing everything about the department, and to answer your question, there is no suicide prevention aide. You are the suicide prevention aide. Stop thinking that we're as fully equipped with the resources the academy taught you. There's supposed to be two officers on the floor in the unit and it's only you, right? So, get it together," Saunders demands.

Tiffany nods in agreement but remains stale faced. Ms. Perry steps away and asks them to follow her out the house to speak to them. They follow.

"I can attest he won't act out here today again. He's not trying to mess up after you've reminded him that he will be out in 2 days. Regardless, still keep a good eye on him. Call me if anything," Ms. Perry advises.

"Yes, ma'am," Tiffany replies.

“Listen, it’s your first day. I came off rough, but like you, I'm a woman in a department where we might be looked at as weak. You’ll realize that we dominate here though. We’re the ones in higher positions, we’re the ones with the promotions, and we maintain order here. We give these young men a motherly figure that they might not have back home. Stay strong, copy?” Warden Saunders comforts Tiffany, her tone apologetic.

“Copy.”

Tiffany walks back towards Inmate Jackson’s cell and peeks in. He casually lies on the floor and listens to his radio, as if nothing has occurred. She continues checking on each inmate, making sure they are alive and well and commences her count. It’s 2:40pm as she waits for her relief officer to come in once roll call breaks. The officer in the A-station bubble buzzes the door, and to her surprise, she is getting relieved by Antonio. He smiles.

“Hey, beautiful! How was your morning shift?” he asks.

“Oh, man, I wouldn't know where to start. I had 30 cell, Jackson I believe his name is, stage a fake suicide attempt for attention and the Warden came, mental health, everyone, and he had me looking dumb because I called it in. Other than that, for it to be the Box, it wasn't as loud or crazy. I guess because they all mostly slept during the first half of my day," Tiffany tells him.

"Oh wow. I hope I don't have to go through anything crazy. I heard it's hectic here, from what my cousin told me."

Another officer comes in through the buzzed gate and relieves the A-station officer. Antonio waves at him, but he doesn't reciprocate.

"I guess it's true what they told us in the academy. We only have our graduating classmates in here. The senior staff hardly speak to us," Antonio continues.

He shrugs his shoulders and receives the keys from Tiffany.

"Tell me about it. The Warden got an attitude with me like it was my fault we are rookies. So messed up," Tiffany agrees.

"Yeah, that's so odd. Well, get home safely and get some rest. Hopefully you don't get stuck for overtime, roll call looked pretty full so you should be fine," he affirms.

"I'm crossing my fingers."

She walks off and leaves the unit.

"Hey, what was your count?!" he yells to her before exiting.

From a distance by the gate she responds, “90! And you're going to have an incoming body to 31 Cell after the count clears!”

Antonio does his house count and walks to the A-station bubble to introduce himself to his partner for the night. CO Fama is a heavy set Italian Guy with a Mafioso demeanor, sporting a big gold chain under his uniform shirt that is barely buttoned.

“What's up, man? Sanchez,” Antonio introduces himself.

Without even a glance, Fama gives him a thumbs up as he writes an entry in the log book. He’s been on this job for years. He’s literally seen it all. At the very beginning of Fama’s career, an inmate snuck a small 2-shooter revolver through the intake area in his rectum, then held another inmate at gunpoint. He’s just waiting for his time to retire, he’s not fazed.

“What's your count, kid?” Fama mumbles while chewing tobacco.

“90, sir. The B-officer I just relieved told me that we should be getting someone new coming in, 31 cell I remember her saying.”

He nods his head and sips his from his coffee mug, “Sounds good. I guess I’ll help you process him in. Take his property, have him sign for it, and only give him the items he's allowed," Fama tells him.

"Yes sir."

"This your first week, huh?" Fama inquires.

"Yes sir, how about you?"

"Kid, I've been here longer than you've been alive. In this specific unit alone I've been the A-officer for over 16 years. I've seen the craziest shit. This unit has actually calmed down with all the new rules, regulations, and polices they've implemented," he chuckles.

Antonio's eyes widened with surprise, "Yeah, I heard. My cousin works in this building and she has told me stories."

"The other Sanchez I am assuming?"

"Yes sir, do you know her?"

"Yeah, I remember when she first started, too. She didn't take no shit from these guys, they respected her and she ran a smooth shift. Let's try to do the same here, okay?"

"Yes sir, definitely," Antonio agrees.

The phone rings, Fama answers.

"Okay, he's coming now? Gotcha."

He hangs up and spits the tobacco into a clear water bottle. Antonio watches as the brown thick liquid flows down to the bottom. He's disgusted.

"Well, 31 cell's on his way. I know this inmate very well. Big time blood guy in this building, always doing stints here in the Box, smokes like crazy, and very disrespectful. He feels like he runs everything. You ready?" Fama looks at him.

"Yes sir."

Two officers and a captain arrive at the main gate escorting Dollar. Antonio squints but doesn't realize who the inmate is right away. The door buzzes and he walks in, cuffed to the front clutching a prayer rug.

"His property will arrive later after chow. For now, just escort him to the cell. You got it from here?" the escorting officer tells Antonio.

Shocked that he knows exactly who the inmate is, Antonio stares at him as sternly as possible. Dollar gives off the same look and grins. He grips the middle of the handcuffs behind Dollar's back and guides him towards his cell. Inmate Jackson, his neighbor, laughs through the opening of his cell.

"Ahhhh! What's popping, blood?" Jackson greets.

"Who is that?" Dollar questions.

"Never do that! It's 730, bro bro! What the fuck you do now, fool?" Jackson tells him through the cell.

"Dumb shit, bro. I'll tell you later. Let me get situated. I don't want this rookie ear hustling anyway."

Antonio locks him in and gives Fama the signal to close the cell door from inside the bubble. He opens the food slot with his key and Dollar extends his arms out to have his cuffs removed. Dollar is released, but before closing the slot he peeks through the opening.

"Yo Sanchez, make sure I get my property before the night ends please. I'm not going to be a problem, that's my word."

Antonio nods, "I got you. I'll call for it after chow, cool?" he assures.

He shuts the slot close before Dollar can even respond.

Antonio's stomach begins to turn, remembering the first time he met Dollar. He walks away and goes about his shift. Time passes and Antonio is walking with the inmates designated to serve dinner up and down the corridor, making sure everyone gets their meal and is properly given a tray, opening and closing slot after slot. He gets to Dollar's cell and opens. Dollar hands him a folded piece of paper. Antonio is nervous.

"Sanchez, was that my property that just came in before chow?"

"Um yeah, I believe it was. I guess once I'm done with the trays I'll sort it out and hand it to you."

Dollar nods and gives him a wink through the door.

The food pantry inmates exit the unit and dinner is over. Antonio walks over to Fama at the bubble and Fama hands him a property receipt form to fill out.

"Hey kid, fill this out. There's a number indicated next to every item. It's up to your discretion what he can and can't have. I don't give a shit, honestly. His stuff is in the search room by the shower. Make sure he gets a copy and you sign it, too," Fama reminds him.

"Gotcha."

He walks over to the room. Dollar has 4 garbage bags full of clothes, sneakers, books, magazines, and food. Antonio puts on his gloves and begins sifting through everything, searching for weapons, contraband, and items not allowed in the unit that normally would be allowed in the general population.

He remembers the small folded paper he was handed. It reads:

"YO LET JU KNOW I'M IN THE BOX FOR 60 DAYS. TELL HER YOU KNOW WHAT'S UP WITH THE SITUATION IF U HAVEN'T ALREADY. LET'S GET THIS MONEY TOGETHER SINCE SHE'S OUT, SHE'LL TELL YOU WHAT AND HOW TO DO IT."

Antonio is taken aback. He's angry and scared at the same time. Not knowing what to do, he rips up the paper and continues looking through the property bags. As if things couldn't get worse, he sifts through the envelopes and looks through all Dollar's pictures. Most of them are naked women, pictures of Dollar with strippers at clubs. Then he realizes a picture of Dollar and his cousin Julissa kissing him on the cheek. Antonio begins to shake.

CO Fama walks into the search room.

"Sanchez, you good? You taking forever and I need you on the floor. We had that guy with the noose earlier on the 7-3 shift. I can't explain you not being there, the cameras are rolling 24/7 in this unit."

"I got you, I'm, umm…done. I'm just writing the property receipt to give him, coming now, sir."

"Got you, the officer relieving us just walked in so you know the unwritten rule, rookies go to lunch first. Matter fact, just go take your meal break now. I'll bring this to him."

"Alright, umm, yeah…I'll go right now," Antonio says.

Antonio walks out and hands over his keys and radio to the officer waiting for him to go on break. He gets buzzed out the unit and heads straight to the locker room. He knows he needs to get in contact with his cousin Julissa and get to the bottom of everything that has been going on.

Julissa is on the phone with her Aunt Ana.

"Juli! I'm sorry to bother you, but Diego got arrested when he went to report downtown at parole. He called me from bookings, he doesn't even know what for! He said he's being targeted for nothing and his parole officer doesn't want to give me any information."

Julissa rolls her eyes and huffs. "There's nothing I can do, Titi. I'm only a correction officer not a police officer, and to be honest he just came home and you still baby him like he's an angel. I understand that's your son, I understand that's my cousin, but I'm not even trying to be involved with his bullshit."

"Okay, but if you see him at work please find out for me, Juli. He's changed a lot just…please," Ana pleads.

"Okay, Titi, I'll let you know. Does Tony know? Because he's at work right now, even though he doesn't have his phone on him, he'll probably check it on his break like I taught him to."

She walks to her couch and lights a cigarette.

"Yes, I've been texting him and told him. He loves his brother so maybe he will find out."

"Okay Titi, speak to you later. I'm really busy right now, ok. If I get any info, I will call immediately," Julissa says in a passive tone.

She hangs up and continues smoking. She goes to text Antonio and leaves him a message.

"Your beautiful brother got locked up again. He must hate being a free man. Call me once your shift is over. Your mom is going nuts again."

Her phone vibrates and it's Antonio. Her face screws up with surprise.

"Tony? What the fuck? You're off?" she questions, looking at the time he's calling. She knows he shouldn't have his cell phone on post even though everyone does. He's too new to do so.

"I just took my meal break and came to the locker room to check my phone and you texted me...and," he explains while on the other line.

She cuts him off, “Well, did you read it? He’s bugging for real. I don't know why he involves himself in shit with no regard for anything,” she states upset.

Antonio looks around the locker room and steps into the bathroom stall before answering.

“Damn, yeah I don't know what's up with him. Maybe it’s a misunderstanding, but um, anyway, me and you really need to talk like ASAP!” he whispers.

“Are you okay? Tell me now!” she questions.

“I'm good. I'm more so just worried about you and I wouldn’t want you getting into shit like Diego.”

“What the fuck are you referring to Tony?”

“I'm coming straight to your house after work tonight, if I don’t get stuck with overtime,” he continues to whisper.

“Umm ok, just call me prior. I was supposed to be here with a friend, but I’ll be here. You’re making me nervous by the way.”

“Trust me, I'm even more nervous. Love you, see you later. I’m going back now,” he warns.

He hangs up on her and walks to the bench directly in front of his locker and looks at himself in the mirror. Dreading to have to go back and get confronted by Dollar about the message, he gathers himself and takes a few bites of his granola bar before heading back upstairs.

Union President Neil Simmons and two of his staff members walk into central bookings demanding to see their correction brother CO Dawson. They heard the news through an inside source at the NYPD who called Neil about one of his beloved correction officers discharging his weapon against an unarmed assailant inside his own home last night. Neil storms in wanting answers and Dawson's side of the story.

"Lieutenant! Where is Dawson! And he better be in his own cell away from everyone else!" Simmons demands from the NYPD Lieutenant.

The Lieutenant points to the holding cell from his desk. Simmons sees Dawson crunched over at the very corner of the cell. He takes out his car key and clinks it along the rusted grey bars, getting his attention.

"Dawson, you okay? How are they treating you? The lawyer is meeting us here right now. Don't speak to anyone. You hear me?" he asks.

Dawson sits alongside the bars, distressed and confused, "Yes, I know. Neil, man…I was defending myself, man. That's all I was doing, defending myself. He was beating up my baby girl. I just blacked out," Dawson pleads.

Simmons listens and can smell the alcohol on his breath as Dawson explains himself secretly.

"D, let me ask you something and I need you to keep it real with yourself before you answer and keep it real with me. Were you under the influence last night?" he whispers.

Dawson's face shows his embarrassment, and he breaks down into tears, "Yes sir."

Simmons takes a step back and looks at the two union staff members behind him, inhales hard and leans in close to the cell bars. Simmons and Dawson graduated the academy back in the late 80s. They were sent to different facilities but would catch each other at department events. Simmons gets a flashback of when Dawson's wife passed away from breast cancer and he made sure to collect some money for the funeral. This hits home for Simmons.

"Don't worry, D. The union is behind you and we'll get you out of this mess. Just bear with us and tell the union lawyer every single detail of what transpired last night, ok?"

"Yes, sir."

"We will be at your arraignment today and we'll take it from there. Hopefully there's bail and we can fight this from the outside, ok? We got your back man, we love you!" he assures him as he continues to sob quietly.

Dawson extends his hand through the bars and tightly squeezes Simmons hand, looking at him with fear dead in his eyes, he nods quietly. As Simmons and his team walk off and pass the other cells in central booking holding multiple offenders awaiting arraignment, Diego paces back and forth waiting to get back on the payphone. The older gentleman before him hangs up and he cuts in front of the person who was supposed to be next. He dials quickly and taunts the guy to step back.

"Please pick up, man!" he tells himself out loud.

The person on the opposite end answers.

"YO?"

"Dice, what's up, bro? It's Diego, where are you at?"

"I'm home, bro. Where you calling me from?" his friend Dice asks on the other line.

"Nah, man, I'm in central bookings. Listen to me, I went to parole and they said I had a warrant, like some federal hold or some shit. I'm going to Rikers till the DEA agents come for me. I won't have bail because I'm on parole so bail's withdrawn regardless. Do me a favor and go to my mom's house tonight and wait there with my mom till Tony gets home. I need you to tell him what's going on. I'm high classification status when I get to Rikers so I know I'll be housed in his building. Tell him I'm going to send him word once I touch down and to not be alarmed if someone tells him I'm there."

"Ok, I got you. Should I tell Julissa, too? Isn't she on the Island, too?" he asks.

"Man, fuck that bitch. She's a hater, man. Just please put my brother on and try to calm my mom down while you there," Diego reminds him.

"I got you, man. You know I start my city bullet next Monday, right? I have to give these motherfuckers a punk ass 8 months. I have to turn myself in and I'll be on the Island after next week, so we might link in there. You know what's up."

"Oh shit, I forgot about all that. Well, do me this solid and if anything, send me a kite once you touch down and I'll do the same."

"Alright, bro, got it. See you soon then."

Diego hangs up and takes a seat on the bench waiting his turn to get seen by the judge.

Back at Rikers, Jackson paces back and forth after receiving his daily medication from the clinician. His mental state is triggered and he starts hearing voices and awkward noises. Jackson spits out the eights pills into the toilet and flushes it. He begins to scream in a state of rage and throws his paperwork and books all over his cell in agony. Dollar bangs on his wall to get his attention.

"Yo! You good man?" Dollar shouts at his door.

Jackson continues to scream. The meal relief officer pays it no mind.

"YO, CO! 30! Cell! 30! Cell! CO!" Dollar yells down the tier.

The screaming stops, but Dollar still yells for the CO because Jackson has not responded. CO Fama walks out the staff bathroom and hears what's going on and walks over. Inmate Jackson is seen hanging from the same noose he had earlier which should have been taken away from him. Fama runs back to the bubble and tells the meal relief officer to open 30 cell and press the alarm.

"Open 30!" Fama yells and signals to the meal relief officer in the A-station.

He runs to the open cell with his 911 knife in an attempt to cut the noose loose and free Jackson before it's too late.

Down by the locker room, Antonio walks up the stairs and the alarm sounds off before he gets to the top.

"Wow, saved by the bell," he silently tells himself.

He stands by the gate and watches while the response team suits up and attends to the affected area. Unbeknownst to him, it's his housing area. Security Captain Davis calls Antonio over through the other gate.

"Sanchez! You're the B officer in the box today, right?" Captain Davis questions.

"Yes sir."

"You have any idea what this alarm could be? Or who?" he interrogates.

"No sir."

Dollar watches as medical personnel and officers escort Inmate Jackson out of his cell on a gurney stretcher. He shakes his head and lies down on the bed, hoping Antonio will come back and speak to him regarding the kite he gave him to read and with an update on his property. He hears the gate open and peeks through the side of his cell. Antonio walks in from lunch.

"Officer Sanchez, can I holla at you please?" Dollar demands.

The alarm clears and Antonio walks into the search room before acknowledging his call from Dollar, but grabs his property and drags the items towards his cell. When he arrives, they stare at each other through the Plexiglas.

"Listen, man, you have more items than what's allowed in the Box, so I put those in your property locker and you'll receive them once your days here are over and you return to population, which is in 60 days or so, I believe."

Dollar could not care less about what's being explained. He quietly whispers, "Did you read it?"

Antonio looks around to make sure no one is in ear shot. Even though there are 90 inmates around them, the next inmate is eight cells away.

"Yeah, I'll let her know. I'm going to cuff you, you're going to step out once the cell opens and grab your bag, then the cell is going to close and I will remove the cuffs through the food slot. You understand?" he tries to say with confidence.

"Come on, man, I'm not new to this shit, you are. I know protocol better than you player, just give me my stuff and holla at Juli for me."

Antonio looks at him like he has three heads, surprised that he just called her by her first name, as if having a picture of the two of them wasn't enough of a surprise. Antonio gives a signal to the officer in the bubble and Dollar retrieves his items then the cell door is locked. He opens the food slot and Dollar sticks his palms out to have the cuffs taken off. He bends down and looks at Antonio through the port.

"I could make us a lot of money, man, just follow what I'm telling you. Juli will break it down for you, she's been doing this for years. Also, tell your brother I send my love. I heard he just came home. That's the big homie," Dollar continues.

Antonio closes the slot in his face mid-conversation. He steps away and checks on the other inmates as if he wasn't just told all that information.

Captain Davis comes into the unit with two other officers trailing behind him. Antonio is on the opposite end of the tier but sees them walking straight to Dollar's cell to speak to him. Antonio walks over. He wants to show face to prove to them he's in tune and has his unit ran tightly.

"Sanchez, you heard what happened?" Captain Davis questions as he sticks his thumbs into his utility belt.

"Yes sir, Jackson had a suicide attempt the minute I left for my meal break."

"Did he show any signs of distress when you were doing your tours prior to?"

"No sir."

CO Fama walks in and makes his way to them.

"What's up, Capt.?" Fama coughs, clearing his throat.

"Fama, you good, right?"

"Yeah, once Sanchez left and Jackson received medication, he decided he would try to kill himself thinking no one would be walking and checking the cells. The crazy part is 31 cell, umm…what's your last name, kid?" Fama knocks on Dollar's cell.

"Parker..." Dollar informs him.

Davis looks in, "Oh, Parker's here, what a surprise," Davis glances around the cell making sure everything is intact and that he doesn't possess any items he shouldn't.

"What's up, Captain D? Yeah, I called Fama because I heard the commotion from Jackson's cell and figured something was wrong," Dollar explains.

Fama nods in agreement and they all look at each other.

"So you prevented a suicide, Mr. Parker?"

"I definitely did, and I would appreciate it if you could speak to the Warden and cut my days by more than half please. You know I do more good than bad here, man, please. The reason I'm here isn't even my fault, I didn't do shit. Remember I found Officer Sanchez when she passed out a few days ago. I'm over saving you and shit. Get me out of here man, please."

He continues to plead his case as Captain Davis nods and listens to everything he's saying.

"He's got a good case captain," Fama suggests.

"I will speak to Warden Brown about your so-called good guy behavior to possibly cut your Box time. I don't know about half, but maybe an earlier release."

Antonio stands to the side listening to how Dollar has these guys wrapped around his finger, including his cousin.

"I'll try to see him before I head out today, I'm transferring to Investigations next week, so I won't be the security captain thereafter, but I'll request it," Davis informs.

"I appreciate that Capt. Congrats on the promotion, I'll see you later," Dollar walks away from the cell door.

Davis and his team walk off and Fama hands over an emergency pin button for Antonio to put on his hip.

Later on that night, Captain Mitchell gets out of the shower, drying off, preparing to leave. Her boyfriend Sean pours himself another glass of liquor on their bed. They have the night to themselves, but she gets a phone call from the headquarters office about work. Their night at home is cancelled.

"Let me jump in the shower really quickly," Sean tells her.

"Sean, I have bad news..."

He undresses and continues to sip from his cup already displaying a buzz.

"I was asked by my Warden to go to the headquarters office," she slowly tells him.

"Are you fucking kidding me, man?! Why the fuck you wait till now to tell me this. I just bought another bottle for us, fuck!" he angrily shouts.

"It's going to be till 7am. I won't get stuck doing overtime and I won't be on the Island. No inmate contact, just logging in the officers that call out for the shift," she convinces him.

Sean sucks his teeth and starts drinking straight from the bottle.

"Whatever, bitch!" he's furious.

"I'm not trying to drain all my vacation time, Sean. Remember we still have the cruise planned next month. We'll have plenty of time to get nasty then, just bear with me. Also, Leah will be with her grandmother down south after next week," she softly tells him, caressing his face.

"Whatever, man," he says under his breath.

She kisses Sean and slowly gets dressed. She places her arm in its sling from her shoulder injury. Sean doesn't even shower; he lies in bed with his alcohol.

"No school tomorrow, so don't worry about Leah waking up early. Just make sure you guys have a good breakfast. I'll be back around 8," she hands him a $50 bill, "Here. Order something from the diner tomorrow."

Captain Mitchell grabs her keys and unlocks her personal weapon from the small safe in the closet and holsters in. She leaves and locks the door.

"Fuck you!" Sean yells one last time once the door locks.

He walks over to the freezer after she leaves and opens the second bottle, and starts to drink from it straight. After a few minutes he sits in the living room and starts to watch porn from his phone, stroking himself. He stops and calls someone unknown to meet him in the hallway.

Within minutes, the doorbell rings. Sean walks to it and looks through the peephole, a guy with a blue hoodie waits. He opens the door and hands the guy $50. The guy passes Sean a small Ziploc. He locks the doors and goes straight to the bathroom. Sean begins to roll up his marijuana and sprinkles the yellowish dust from the Ziploc.

He lights it and gets an instant rush. High as a kite, he continues to watch porn from his phone. It's not really doing much for him, but the blunt feels euphoric, a hallucinating feeling he can't control. He steps into Leah's room to check in on her.

His mind is racing and he can't seem to control his sexual urge. He lies next to Leah and slowly begins to touch her backside while stroking himself. He's not as conscious as he wants to be. Sean gets up and attempts to penetrate her vaginal area.

Warden Brown pours himself a drink while some soft jazz plays in the background. He awaits his female companion; he hears the door knock. Captain Mitchell walks in completely dressed in the opposite of what she had on previously, wearing a short and beige dress and heels. She leans in and they begin to kiss passionately, the door closes.

Antonio walks into his apartment and opens the door. His brother's friend Juan Ramos aka Dice, his mother, and her boyfriend Roberto are smoking cigarettes in the living room. Dice is a tall slender, heavily tattooed male.

Antonio cautiously drops his book bag and removes his work boots by the door.

"Tony! How was your day, papa?" his mom asks.

"It was fine. What are you guys doing?" he questions.

"What's up, Tone? I haven't seen you in a minute, but congrats on the new job," Dice extends his hand for a shake.

"Yeah, thanks," Antonio blandly responds.

He walks to the kitchen and pours himself some juice, "What's going on? You guys are acting weird."

"Well, baby, Diego was arrested earlier for a warrant he says. I called Julissa to help me get to the bottom of it. Diego has been calling non-stop, but has no idea what's going on. Dice came to speak to you about how you can figure out what to do and calm me down because you know how I get with my anxiety and high blood pressure," Ana explains worriedly.

"Yeah, man, you know Diego and you guys are like family so I just wanted to holla at you, Tony," Dice explains.

Antonio stands bothered. After a semi-hectic shift, he just wanted to come home, shower, and sleep.

"Let's go talk privately, bro. Your room or my car or whatever," Dice offers.

Dice stands up and they head towards the room.

"What the hell's going on, Dice?"

"Listen, man, Diego got jammed up. Had a gun on him and coke when he got pulled over. Your mom thinks it's an old warrant because that's what he keeps telling her. Long story short, he won't get bail because he's on parole, but he told me to come here and put you on so when he gets to the Island you can look out for him."

"Look out for him? What the fuck can I do? I literally just started. I have no pull in there. The only person I have in there is Julissa, and she's out for the next few weeks," he reverts.

"Exactly. Call her, tell her to teach you what to do, and you can give your brother shit to be able to move while he's in there," his attempt to make sense is weak.

"Move what? Wait, what? You're not making any sense!" Antonio starts to get agitated.

"Okay. I'm done sugarcoating shit, bro. Julissa brings in Tobacco, weed, and mad other shit to her boyfriend in there. She also did it for Diego when he was fighting his case. She got paid, he got paid, he helped you with bills and everyone eats off it. You could make a killing if you do the same."

Antonio freezes.

"Call her and call her out on it. I'll bet you she'll be honest about it. He told me to ask you to help him, since he's always helped you. He gave you an almost brand-new car Tony, just look out for your family, bro," he continues pleading.

Dice walks out the door. Antonio changes from his cargo pants into some shorts, grabs his car keys, and leaves the house. Everyone in the living room sits there confused. Antonio gets into his car and heads over to Julissa to get to the bottom of what Dollar and Dice have told him.

Antonio gets out of the elevator and calls Julissa for the 4th straight time since he's left the house. She has not answered or replied to any of his texts. He knocks.

"Who is it?!" says Julissa from another room.

"It's Tony!"

Getting up she looks through the peephole and unlocks her door chain, "Tony? What's going on? Are you okay? Why are you here?" she doesn't fully open the door and is barely peeking out.

"We really need to talk, Juli. People are saying things about you and I'm trying not to believe rumors, but I also see shit and I just want to get to the bottom of this before it's too late. You feel me?" he pleads.

"This is not a great time, Tony. It's late, I've been drinking, and I have someone over and I just can't," she sucks her teeth.

A voice from inside asks, "Ju, are you okay? Who's that?"

Julissa sighs and opens the door fully exposing her in a white robe and her male companion behind her who is also in a white robe. To Antonio's surprise, it's Neil, the correction officers' Union President he met at his graduation.

"You ordered food, Juli?" he questions.

"Neil, that's my cousin, remember? From the last graduating class, I introduced you guys."

"Oh, shit. I'm so sorry, man, my apologies. You look totally different outside your uniform and hat," Simmons gathers himself and his robe.

Antonio stands firm not saying a word. There's an awkward silence for about 20 seconds.

"Juli, I'ma head out. I'll see you some other time. Family issues first, tend to your cousin, okay?"

Julissa rolls her eyes as Neil walks back and begins to dress himself. She lets Antonio in and they shake hands on his way out. He awkwardly closes the door behind him. Julissa and Tony walk towards the couch. She hands him a water bottle from her personal at home bar stand.

"What's going on, Tony? You're being sus and more weird than usual," Julissa shakes her head.

"I'm going to just ask you something straight up, Ju. You know I will never want you to think I'm judging you or looking at you in a different way. The reason I even had the thought of being a correction officer is because of you. I've watched you grow and build. You worked retail and then worked at the airport and now look at you. Beautiful condo, beautiful car, you go on vacations, shopping sprees, you're living life," Antonio tells her.

She cuts him off mid-sentence, "Thanks, Tony, but cut to it already..."

"Are you bringing drugs to Parker? That inmate, the one who works for you in the kitchen, you know who I'm talking about?" he spurts out.

"Yes I know who you're talking about, Tony. To answer your question, yes, yes I have.
"Did you see me do it or has someone on the Island spread a rumor and you overheard it?" she questions him.

"No! No one except him, who told me straight up, and well, Dice, Diego's boy told me tonight, too," Antonio claims.

"Dice!? That bum ass jailbird? Where and why the fuck is he telling you this shit?" she demands.

Antonio gets up and is overly nervous, "I don't know, Juli, but please tell me what the fuck is going on? Why are you doing that? And why do these guys know? Aren't you scared of getting caught or them switching on you and telling the higher ups on you? This is dangerous. You could lose your job, even get arrested!"

Julissa's blood starts to boil, "I know all of this, Tony! Since I have been gone, I've contemplated stopping. Dollar is an old boyfriend of mine. At first, I did it just to help him out.

"Why would you risk it all, all you've worked for?" Antonio is concerned.

Now she's frustrated, "Stop judging me, Tony! You don't understand what I go through! Or how real it gets in there! You're just starting, it's easy to judge from the outside in, but you have no idea. If you saw your mom on the Island tomorrow, suffering, not knowing her fate, no one being able to be there for her emotionally, physically, and you were able to bring her a Bible or outside food, would you?"

"I mean, yeah, that's my mom. I would do anything for her."

"Well, exactly. I love Dollar, so please don't judge me. Listen, I would never want you to have to be in that predicament, but you'll start to see people from your building, your neighborhood, your old high school, even family like I have, come in and out of the Island. We're human, we sympathize and we act on that even when it's against the rules. When your brother was there fighting his case, I looked out for him. He paid his lawyer off and sent money to you guys with my help. I also benefited financially. Just know it's an unwritten rule in there for COs to look out for certain people. It's wrong, but sometimes it's inevitable. That's all I have to say about this," she explains.

Antonio sits back down and is at a loss for words.

"I was talking to Neil, as you saw, prior to you interrupting. He's moving out of the Island and I'll be working at the union office once I get cleared to come back so those days for me are over anyway. I'm done," there is relief in her voice.

"Wow, really? Congrats. Well, I hope you are done. I'm tired of seeing friends and family getting locked up, and I can't fathom you in that same position," he shakes his head.

"Yes, Tony, I'm done."

They get up off the couch and hug each other. Still holding his hands, she looks at him dead in the eyes. The soft R&B music is still playing in the background.

"Tony, a word of advice: If you're going to do something wrong, make sure you do it right."

Antonio nods and walks over to the door, waves goodbye, and heads out. Julissa shakes her head and pours herself another glass, locking her door.

A FEW DAYS LATER

CO Mohammad is seated on the B-side while making a log book entry. He makes sure his count is clear and everything in the housing area appears to be secure. His A-bubble station Officer is CO Cassandra Garçon, a young and energetic Haitian female with a different wig for every day of the week, long nails, and well set makeup. Her main objective is to do her eight hours and run out the gate just so she can party and enjoy her second job (the nightlife). She is seated, writing in her log book, counting razors, and doing other paperwork.

"B-officer! What's your name again?!" she shouts at him obnoxiously while tapping the glass.

Mohammed drops his logbook, startled, and walks over to the bubble, "Mohammed, ma'am, and you are?"

"Ma'am?! Are you blind? I'm younger than you, sir! Did you just start? And what's your count? I just came back from Miami Memorial Day, so I'm still tipsy and deaf from all the loud music and free drinks," she tells him.

Mohammed has the "don't know what to answer first face."

"Are you deaf, too, Mohammed?" she questions.

"No, sorry. Um, yes, I am fairly new. The count's 59, 30 on the B-side and 29 on the A. All appears secure."

Garçon turns up the radio once he finishes speaking. In her world, she runs the show and no officer fresh out of the academy is going to alter that. She's only been on the job for two years, but her street savviness is of an original gangster.

"Yoooo! This is my song! Anyways, we going to have a steady shift. This isn't my steady house, but I get put here often. All the inmates here know my routine and they all obey what I ask of them, so just keep control, make sure they not cutting or jumping anyone, change their hot pot water so they can make their soup and stuff and we can both skate out of here on time. I'm going to the strip club tonight and no one's getting in my way. Not you, not these inmates, not any mandated overtime, nooooooneeee! Copy?" she shouts through the music.

"Yes, will do!" Mohammad smiles as he admires her rules.

Garçon yells, "ON THE LOCKOUT!!" and begins to open every cell door from the electronic knobs inside the A-station bubble. The inmates walk out holding their coffee cups, radios, and other miscellaneous items in hand. She turns on the TV and as the inmates get on the phone and/or walk into the dayroom area, they greet her.

"Hey, Ms. G!"

"What's up, Ms. G!"

CO Mohammad watches and walks around the unit making sure everyone locks out, and those who remain in their cells are given one last chance before the option to lockout is over.

"Last call on the lockout, fellas! Get what you need! Last call! Next lockout is at 5pm! No exceptions!" Mohammad shorts with authority.

Inmates laugh and snicker amongst themselves, calling him a clown and bozo under their breath. He notices two inmates from the other night who witnessed him being splashed with urine and nods at them. They shake their heads and go on the phone. Dice, who just got in last night from turning himself in, remains half way out of his cell gathering food from other inmates welcoming him.

"Come on 8 cell, option's over. Ms. G's about to lock the doors," he warns.

"I'm coming, big dawg, I just got in. Give me a few, I'm starving, please," Dice pleads.

"Okay, hurry up. The Captain should be making her rounds any minute and I want to clear the corridor before she or he does."

"I got you, man, I run this house. You gonna be fine. I'ma clean my cell once she walks though, please. This shit is dirtier than a mothafucka," Dice explains.

"No problem," Mohammad seems understanding.

Dice and Mohammad signal to Garçon that she can lock the cell. They walk side by side towards the dayroom passing the bubble.

"Ms. G, what's poppin?" Dice greets Garçon with the same Ebonics as blood gang member greeting a fellow blood gang member.

"Hi, Ramos, you back again? You don't get tired of this shit, huh?" she responds sarcastically.

"I am tired, Ms. G. The precinct hates me and stay pinning me for bullshit. I turned myself in on this BS ass sale they had me for, so I have a city bullet to do which is 8 months along with a 1-3 years state time that I'm getting sentenced for next month."

"Copy. Once everything settles, you clean the cell. I could smell that shit when I came in to do my count," she assures him.

"I was just telling the new CO," Dice agrees.

She gives him the thumbs up and Dice walks into the dayroom, giving noticeable gang handshakes to all his peers. This in and out of jail is part of the game to him and many others. After a while, they develop normalization to this world. They congregate here with other guys they wouldn't normally catch in their neighborhood, but have a friendship and bond with while behind these walls.

"Mohammad, you good over there?" Garçon checks in. She might seem cavalier at first, but she truly cares about everyone's wellbeing, be it her inmates or her staff. Everyone gets respect and empathy until they cross her.

"Yes, everything's cool. You okay?" he reverts.

"Told you I'm chilling. Look at this job as being in a bad neighborhood, the only difference is you maintain order, be yourself, don't disrespect anyone, and move with confidence. You'll be fine. Also, the captain's next door. Make sure shit's on point," she advises.

"Copy:"

The door buzzes and Captain Davis walks in and enters the A- station looking at the housing area on both sides making sure things are in order. He knows who's who and what rank, if any, they hold within the house or the jail in its entirety. Captain Davis was a Gang Intelligence Officer for many years before transferring to security. He's savvy when it comes to tattoos, code words, and handshakes. He walks into every housing area to dissect everyone individually.

"Officer Garçon, welcome back," he smiles as he opens the A-station door.

"Big D! How are you feeling?" Garçon flirts away.

"I'm doing well, transferring to the Inspector General's office soon," he boasts.

"Oh, so you're going to be investigating, cracking down on your own people, huh?"

"Well, yes and no. If they're not doing the wrong things, they shouldn't have to worry about me, right?"

"Unh huh! Anyways, Mohammad! Captain's here! Bring your log book to sign!" she shouts out forgetting which side of the housing area Mohammad is on.

Captain Davis steps out the bubble and Garçon buzzes the door open to the B-side where Mohammed is. He salutes him.

"Good evening, Captain! How are you?" Mohammad clears his throat.

"Good. How'd your day start? More importantly, how are you doing mentally, from the incident a few nights ago?" he questions him, knowing that the urine splashing can cause an emotional and mental strain on anyone.

"I took it with a grain of salt, sir. I'm using that experience to conduct certain situations and access them differently, in hopes they won't happen again," he explains.

They both walk up the corridor and continue conversing. The inmates know that Captain Davis isn't one to play with so they remain still and quiet as he makes his rounds.

"Good way of looking at things. Remember, a lot of these guys are here for not following rules implemented in society, many are even here because there's a chemical imbalance and they can't function simply, so be mindful," he reminds Mohammad.

"Yes sir."

They get buzzed back out and enter the A-side of the housing area, "You seem level headed, just make sure it's consistent and you'll do fine," Captain Davis salutes.

"Yes sir, absolutely."

The captain enters the A-station and signs the books and leaves the housing area. Dice patiently waits for CO Mohammad to return back to his side to open up the slop sink and obtain some cleaning material to clean his cell, now that the coast is clear.

"Hey, you can open the slop sink and let Ramos gather shit to clean his smelly ass cell. Once he's done, chow should be here and they can serve the food. This house doesn't go out, they eat in house, since it's high classification," Garçon informs him.

"Okay, yeah, sounds good."

Mohammad shuffles for the keys and opens the door. Dice grabs a mop bucket, broom, and cleaning spray and walks to his cell. Mohammad follows to supervise his every move.

"Damn, CO, you're gonna watch me the entire time?" Dice questions him with confusion.

"Well, yeah, just want to make sure you give back all the supplies and don't keep anything you're not supposed to have," Mohammad contests.

"The academy teaches you guys good I see. I have family on the job, I know what's up, I respect it," he chuckles.

"Oh yeah?"

Dice enters his cell while Mohammad watches from outside. Giving Garçon a head nod, he wants her to notice he's on top of things and running the tight shift asked of him in the very beginning of their meet and greet.

"Yo, a few days ago you got splashed in 5 main, right? On the midnight shift…you ever find out who violated you like that?" Dice reminds him of the incident.

"Wait, what? Who told you this? Matter of fact, how did you know? You told me you just got in last night?" he questions with embarrassment.

"Word travels quick here, big dawg. Rikers isn't as big as you think it is, especially for a person like me who comes in and out this bitch. I know who does what and with who, what COs are assholes, the cool ones, the gang affiliated officers, everyone!"

"Gang affiliated officers? That's an oxymoron isn't it?" Mohammad inquires more.

"Listen, man, 90% of COs are minorities, like you and I right?"

He stops and looks at him dead in his eyes.

"We all come from the same neighborhoods, only difference is you took a test and we didn't. Most COs is just as gangster as some inmates I know. Look at Ms. Garçon, she's a sweetheart, but she's blood affiliated. She probably doesn't bang like that, but she's well known in Brooklyn. That's why cats respect her shit here," Dice continues to break it down.

"Yeah, I've noticed," Mohammad agrees.

"What I'm trying to get at is, basically, if you want respect here, you got to earn that shit. It's not given. I'ma keep it a buck with you. I, personally, can handle the inmate who threw piss in your face," he assures.

"How the hell can you do that?"

"I know exactly who did it. He's blood, too, so I can even make him apologize to you and have other cats in here put some respect on your name. You'll never have to go through some crazy shit like that ever again."

Mohammad steps in the cell a little and continues to listen. Lured in by what's being said to him, he doesn't even realize he's crossing a boundary.

"You have 20 more years left in this bitch, have it be a smooth one. I can handle that for you. Think about it and let me know what's up. Everyone here knows me. I'm credible, ask around, but this will be between us, you heard," he reminds him.

"So, what would you want from me? Since you're over here offering services, what's the catch?" he chuckles.

"Honestly, I have a bad tobacco habit. Just throw me a few loose Newport's here and there. I know you smoke, I can see the pack of cigarettes poking out from your left cargo pocket."

Mohammad looks to his left and sees the top of the pack visibly noticeable and popping out.

"That's it, huh?"

Dice continues to clean and nods yes. Picking up all the supplies, he steps out his cell and Ms. Garçon locks it from the bubble. They walk back to the front of the housing area and Mohammed reaches into his pocket and slowly retrieves a loose cigarette and clutches it in one hand, opening the closet with the other. Dice puts back the supplies and Mohammed quickly throws the loose cigarette on the closet floor. Dice catches on and goes in to pick up.

"Alright, you're done here, right?" he asks, trying to keep everything normal.

"Yes sir."

He locks the slop sink and Dice walks in the dayroom as if everything was normal. Ms. Garçon looks over to Mohammad and checks in on him, not catching what just happened.

"You good, right? Chow's on its way!" she reminds him.

"Yeah, everything's cool..."

On the other side of the building, inmates slowly walk into the gymnasium as the Catholic priest greets and holds small conversations with everyone in attendance. Four correction officers are present at every exit, monitoring everyone. A predominantly Latino crowd of inmates brings the Trinitarios and Latin Kings gangs together to congregate about any problems and drug transactions circulating the building. Shorty walks in handcuffed and escorted by an officer, being placed in the administrative segregation unit due to him being caught with contraband. He is still granted religious services, but will remain segregated from the general population.

With a noticeable busted lip and swollen eye, other inmates walk by him signaling that they know what happened. A fellow Trinitario gang member stands firm in front of Shorty. The escort officer signals him to step back a few feet as he is in charge of Shorty's safety.

"Step back, man. Go over to the population side or I'll have you sent back to your house," the escort officer says.

Shorty interjects.

"I already know, bro. Once I leave admin seg, I'm back on. Tell Flacko we good, just let me get out this situation."

Shorty couldn't care less that the officer is listening to what he has to say. He knows that if he doesn't check in with his gang it can get real really quick. Danny Rios aka Flacko, a tall and slender Hispanic male who sports a French braid with the word "LOYALTY" tattooed on his neck, runs the drugs to other gangs and generates money for himself and those in the Trinitarios. He's not the highest ranking on Rikers Island, but is in charge of everyone in this particular building. He walks in with a few others as service begins. He and Shorty lock eyes.

"In the name of the Father, the Son, and the Holy Spirit," the Catholic Priest announces aloud.

Everyone blesses themselves in unison, even Shorty who's handcuffed to the front and shackled at the waist. The escort officer sees everyone is seated and slowly walks over to the other officer at the exit and they begin to chat briefly about last night's basketball game. Shorty tries to get Flacko's attention. Another inmate notices and taps Flacko on the back and looks over to him. Flacko dismisses the fact that Shorty wants to talk. He didn't get the drugs through to him so he's already a target.

The priest continues to preach and begins to speak verses from the Bible. Shorty feels disrespected. He signals for Flacko to go meet him in the bathroom, knowing the officer has to let him go if he asks.

"CO! Can I use the bathroom please? I can't hold it, man, please. No one's in there right now, let me go really quick!" Shorty begs.

The CO nods no and crosses his arms, "Wait until service is over. You know I can't let you go while the population is still seated here," he reminds Shorty.

Shorty does the unthinkable and begins to pee on himself. The CO can see his grey jumpsuit drip and stain with urine. He has no choice but to let him go.

"What the fuck? Hurry up, man!" the escort officer sucks his teeth.

Shorty walks over slowly enough so Flacko can see he's roaming free towards the bathroom. The officer walks back to the exit and shakes his head laughing at how Shorty just peed on himself. The other two officers become lax and they all begin to talk amongst themselves, disregarding the general population inmates. Flacko shifts and walks slowly into the bathroom.

"Bro, I got something, bro. They only caught the scalpel. Here, take this," he whispers.

He reaches into the semi-jumpsuit and hands him a finger cut from latex gloves full of marijuana and one full of pills. "I boofed this. They didn't catch this."

The term "boof" refers to an inmate placing an impermissible item and concealing it inside their rectum to avoid being detected by the correction officers.

Flacko looks at him unimpressed.

"Listen, call Mya and she'll come to visit you. I'm visitor and phone restricted till I go to court for the scalpel. Make her bring you the bag and we continue making this bread," he assures him.

"You're lucky, bro. We were ready to clap your shit in here," Flacko warns him.

Flacko takes the handmade blade wrapped in tape from his mouth, showing him he was ready for war.

The CO calls from just outside the bathroom stall, "Yo! You good, man!? Come on, we're going back!"

"I'm coming man, I'm coming!"

He walks out and Flacko stays inside the bathroom looking at the drugs.

Diego gets to Rikers Island and has been patiently waiting in the intake area for over 18 hours to be properly housed. He's frustrated and exhausted after being held without bail at his arraignment. He knows he's going to be here for a while until his next court date. In his bullpen are two heroin addicts, a transsexual inmate, and an elderly male in his late 70s. He wants out.

"Yo, CO! What's up with getting housed, man? I've been here for 24 hours!" Diego shouts by the gate.

A random officer looks up from over his desk and stops in the middle of writing something in his log book. He walks over to the pen.

"What's your last name, sir?" a correction officer yells to him.

"Sanchez! Diego Sanchez!"

The officer goes back to his desk and grabs a floor card with Diego's name and picture and information. The card reads "+17 HIGH CLASSIFICATION." He grabs the keys and walks back, unlocking the pen. Another inmate who is an intake worker grabs a set-up containing a towel, bed sheets, soap, and a toothbrush and hands it over to Diego.

"Why are you high classification, Sanchez?" the CO asks while visibly sizing him up.

"This isn't my first dip in the shark pool, man, you know that," Diego reminds him.

"So, I don't have to tell you what's expected from you here, and you're going to act accordingly, I assume?"

"Yeah, man, definitely," he smiles.

They walk through the busy corridor and get to the housing area. Diego looks up and reads "7 MAIN."

"Wow, you brought me to the Trinitario and Crip house, huh?" he asks.

"You're not labeled as a security risk group? You're not affiliated like I asked you when you got off the court bus, right? You responded no, right? So, what's the issue?" the CO interrogates him.

Diego concedes, "Yeah you're right."

He places his set-up items on the floor and ties his sneakers extra tight and begins to stretch. The CO yells "& MAIN" and the door is buzzed open. He hands over Diego's floor card to the A-station officer, CO Tiffany Thompson. As a new jack, most officers experience the worst behaved housing areas on purpose to ensure they can handle any situation.

"Okay, thank you. He's going to the A-side, 20 cell," Tiffany tells the escorting officer and Diego.

The gate buzzes open and he stares down the two inmates on the phone. He walks in and looks on his left and right, passing the dayroom area where there are a few inmates watching a movie. He goes straight to 20 cell, which has already been popped open. He sees there is no mattress so he drops his set-up on the steel bed frame and makes his way back to the dayroom. He gets everyone's attention by banging on the gate.

"Yo, I need a mattress for 20 cell! And I need it by the time I get off the phone, you heard!?"

The inmates watching the movie turn around and look at him like he's crazy. The oldest of the group gets up from his seat and walks out, staring at Diego. They slightly brush shoulders. Another other inmate, Calbo aka Chris Arroyo, a heavier set, bald-headed inmate sporting a decent-sized Cuban link chain and rosary, gets out of his seat and makes his way towards the corner table. He sits with his back against the wall and calls Diego over. Calbo extends his hand for a shake as Diego sits across from him.

"Que lo que mani?" (Translates to what's the word bro?) Calbo greets him.

"Chilling. Who got the crib, you?" Diego questions with authority.

Calbo, in a heavy accent, "Yeah, that's a fact. You know this is a Crip and Trini crib, right? All the Crips went to the barbershop just now, but they'll be back in a minute. I know you blood, but out of respect because you're still Latino I'm going to give you that heads up. You want to move on any of my bros, we do it like men, you come to me. The blues, I don't care about em'. Also, your mattress is in a cell by now, but I doubt you're staying, right?" he recommends with power.

"Yeah, I'm not staying. I'm trying to get to the other side of the building."

"Tato (copy) Do what you got to do, but you already know," he warns respectfully.

Diego gets up and walks towards his cell. He slowly closes the door and takes the top off his toothpaste. He places it at the end of the door to make it seem like it's locked and closes it slowly. He unbuckles his belt and takes out a small scalpel embedded in the buckle area. There is a commotion from the other inmates returning from the barbershop. A few pass his cell, but they haven't noticed him yet. Diego quietly walks out with the scalpel in hand and cuts the inmate to the left of him from behind, slicing his cheek and ear. Blood starts to leak. Caught off guard, his reaction is delayed. Another inmate runs in his cell and they begin to go at it.

"Stop fighting!" Tiffany yells from the bubble. Her B-officer hears the scream and runs to the gate.

Havoc erupts and the Crips become hesitant to approach Diego with his scalpel in hand. One Crip rushes him from behind and they begin to tussle as he grabs a razor from his ass and swings nonstop at Diego's face in an attempt to do the same thing Diego just did to his boy. Calbo speed walks from the dayroom and applies a chokehold on the Crip on top of Diego. The other Crips begin to assemble and overpower the two by punching and kicking Calbo to the ground. He covers his face and the brawl continues to grow as more inmates join the action.

CO Tiffany nervously presses the wrong button inside the A-station in an attempt to get the B-officer who was supervising the inmates on the other side of the housing area. She needs him to get over there to spray the inmates with OC to calm them down until the response team arrives, which can take a few minutes. Her anxiety has her pressing multiple buttons. She presses the food port door that separates the A-side and B-side by accident. The inmates from the B-side take advantage and make their way to where the war began. The back and forth cause inmates from both sides to throw chairs and use brooms and mops against each other and it's a full-blown riot.

Within minutes, the house escalates into a war zone. Inmates throw hot water from the hot pot towards the B-officer on the floor, forcing him to exit the door and seek refuge; him and CO Tiffany run out towards the exit gate of the front of the housing area and await the response team and emergency service unit.

CHAPTER 6

Ana, Antonio's mom, is sound asleep on the bed as Roberto, her boyfriend, slowly wakes up and begins to dress himself. He gathers his clothes and notices that Ana has a small safe on the floor of her closet, and it is slightly opened. He double checks to make sure she's asleep and walks over to it. It is unlocked and it contains a vanilla envelope with cash and some gold jewelry. She had taken it out earlier with hopes of her son Diego being granted bail, but she forgot to lock it up. He takes out the money from the envelope, counts $1,000 and pockets it, placing the envelope back in the safe.

Just as Roberto walks out, Ana wakes up, "Hey, papi, you leaving?"

"Yeah babe, I got to go and get things ready for the tire shop tomorrow, you know?" Roberto claims.

Ana gets off of the bed in an attempt to sexually seduce Roberto into staying longer. She begins to hug and kiss him, but he laughs it off. She unbuttons his pants and notices the ten 100-dollar bills poking out his left pocket.

"Wow, you have money. Let me get something, papa!"

He pushes her away and starts to get irritated when she jokingly begins to take out the bills from his pocket.

"Ana! Stop, get off of me! I have to go, you're still high. Go back to sleep!" he demands.

She doesn't stop and keeps nagging at him, "Baby, just stay please. Let's smoke again. I have a few dollars here, look. Let's smoke. Please, daddy, please come on. Give me. Stay, stay!"

He gets agitated and pushes her off, she lands back on the bed.

"I told you get the fuck off of me, bitch!" he shouts.

"Okay, okay, damn! Go then, leave. You probably stole that money from me anyway. You think I'm stupid?!"

Roberto's blood boils internally and he rages towards her, distributing closed fist blows to Ana's face. He knocks her out and continues beating her face in while she moans in agony.

Mya sits on the toilet and opens a pregnancy test. She's anxious and takes in a deep breath to calm her nerves. Her handshakes as she holds it under her urine in the toilet. She finishes up and places it to her right, on the sink. Her phone vibrates with an incoming call. It's a jail call. She bypasses the automated operator message.

"Yes? Who is this?" she questions.

"What's good? It's Flacko. I'm Shorty's boy. You know he's in the box, right?"

She rolls her eyes, "Yes, I know. Why are you calling me?"

"He told me to holla at you to keep this thing going, and I have a Western Union number for you to pick up your money. There's $1,500 for you. It's yours, just come see me tomorrow. My name is Danny Rios. I'm in the same building and all that, okay?"

"Okay, yeah, I'll be there," she says while shaking her head.

"Okay good, good. Bring all the clothes you can bring, you understand what I'm saying? The white tees and everything else, copy?"

Mya's pretty savvy to the lingo, but she was clearly annoyed by it all, "Yes, okay, I got it."

She hangs up as her life starts to become more unbearable. She flushes the toilet and pulls up her pants, almost forgetting the pregnancy test. She grabs it and it reads (+), indicating that she is pregnant. Her eyes overflow with tears as she looks at herself in the mirror.

The following morning at the 7AM roll call, the officers meet in the gymnasium and wait to be debriefed before going to their assigned housing areas. Antonio's demeanor is off. He has too much going on in his head from the events that have transpired in the last few days. The back and forth with his cousin Juli and the inmate he knows she brings in drugs for and their romantic history, walking in on his mom bruised up from the physical assault by her boyfriend, who is nowhere to be found, the fact that his older brother is roaming around the Island. It's all overwhelming and deteriorating him, mentally and emotionally. All of that has to be put on pause right now as he's about to start his 8-hour shift that can easily become a 16-hour one.

The Captain commences her speech to all her staff, and the people form two lines.

"This is an occupation where being lax can cost you your safety along with the safety of the inmates you supervise. In very few cases, it can cost you your job. The officer who pressed the wrong button, allowing the inmates to go to the other side of the unit where their rival gang might be housed was a detriment to everyone. It got out of hand and became overly violent. The chaos lasted hours before ESU was able to interfere. Six inmates were slashed, one inmate lost his left eye when he was stabbed with a broomstick, one inmate received 2nd degree burns to his face and chest after getting the pot of boiling water thrown in his direction. Luckily, the two officers on post did not get physically hurt, but the one is on suspension leave for her lack of knowledge of protocol. Let's be cognizant, let's assess situations. We all want to leave the same way we came in. Thank you."

CO Mohammad slowly tries to wiggle in roll call without being noticed, he winks at Antonio. Antonio shakes his head.

Captain Davis notices but continues, "CO Smith - 3 main! CO Mercado - dorm 16 B! CO Sanchez - 5 main A! CO Mohammed, fill out a late slip and report to 5 main B!"

They both look at each other as roll call breaks. Mohammed waits for Antonio.

"What's up, bro? How have you been?" Mohammad asks, standing right next to him in line formation.

"Stressed, man. A lot going on, but after today, I'm off for the next three days so I hope they're smooth. Why are you always late, man?"

"Bad habits. I got to improve, I know," Mohammad recognizes.

They walk to the central control window and retrieve their OC sprays together. Mohammad asks for a late slip and they walk towards the housing area.

"I worked here a few days ago as the B-officer, too, even though it's high classification. They didn't give me any issues at all. They saw I was cool and they reciprocated."

"Oh ok. I've never done the A-station. I hate answering the phone. Today is A-Z last names for visits and probably law library for some of them, so I know it's going to be busy as fuck," Antonio complains.

"Well, don't stress any more than you already are. I got the floor on lock, so we should have a good shift, trust me," Mohammad lets him know ahead of time.

They arrive at the gate and yell "5 MAIN!" but no one is in the bubble.

"It's probably Garçon. She's the steady officer here, basically. She's probably doing her count," Mohammad assures Antonio.

"Yo man, remind me to call Tiffany tonight. You know the Captain was referring to her being the one suspended for the whole riot that happened, right?"

"Damn, for real? You know they could fire her, right? I hope she doesn't man; she looks too good," Mohammad jokes.

"You're a clown, bro. Yo, what's up, man? You think everything is okay in there?" Antonio seems worried.

Mohammad takes out his flashlight and flashes it inside to get the officer's attention.

The A-side door opens and Jamel Thomas aka Killah, a tall, dark-skinned athletically built inmate, comes out holding a broom and garbage bag in hand. His only garment is grey basketball shorts and slippers.

"She's coming. She had me cleaning once everyone locked in. They made a mess and you know how she is. Oh shit, Mohammad, you working today?" Killah is peeking from his side of the housing area.

"Yeah, man, I'll be here," Mohammad smiles.

"Damn, they remember you?" Antonio is taken aback.

"Told you I had this house on smash," he boasts.

CO Garçon comes out with garbage in her hand, "What's good, ya?! I'm coming right now. I'm sorry I had you waiting; you know these are my kids. What's up, Mohammad? They got you here again? I don't have to break it down to your partner, right? What's your name?" she questions.

"Sanchez."

She opens the gate and they all walk into the A-station bubble.

"Hi, Sanchez. Well, I'm out. The count is good, trust me. Just lock him in when you can. Matter of fact, let him stay out and watch TV since he helped me with this mess. Let me out. Be safe, ya."

Antonio grabs the keys and lets her out. Killah steps into the B-side of the housing area.

"Hey, man. Aren't you on the A-side?" Antonio questions.

"Yeah I am, but can I go holla at my man real quick? 5 minutes. He has a magazine for me, please," Killah pleads.

"Yeah, go. Hurry up though, the Captain will be walking soon," Mohammad permits.

Killah speed walks up the corridor, stopping at every cell to show how much pull he has.

"Yo, man. You can't be that cool, you saw what happened last night with Tiffany. What if something happens? That's not his designated side," Antonio tells him.

"Don't be a scaredy cat, man. They're locked in, we're good. I told you I got this," Mohammad assures.

Antonio nervously monitors Killah through the gate. Killah grabs a magazine under the cell and rushes back to the bubble.

"Told you, CO, 123. I won't ever play you, man."

"Okay cool, appreciate it."

He buzzes him from one side to the next. CO Mohammed gives him a handshake like they have been best friends for years.

"Are you staying out?"

"Nah, I'm locking in man. I'm going to read this magazine really quick. You good though?" Killah asks.

"Yeah man, chilling. Tell Dice I'm working today and I need him to do chow later."

"Copy! Yo, Sanchez, I got to holla at you on the lockout. It's important," Killah informs him.

"Tell me now because it's going to get busy later. I've never done the A-station," Antonio asserts.

Killah looks at him, "Yo, Diego wrote me a kite. He sends his love, you heard. He's in the Box cause he was involved in that 7 main shit yesterday. I don't know why they put him there. That's the big homie, you guys look alike, too, that's crazy."

Antonio looks shocked and remains blank.

Mohammad interjects, “Yo, Killah, keep it real man. What’s good with you and Ms. G? You gonna hit that when you get out of here, huh?”

“Gangster’s don’t talk much, man. Sit your ass down, I’ll see you in a bit. Sanchez, open my cell!” Killah follows in a secretive but jokingly matter.

Killah walks away and locks into his cell.

“Yo, I know he be hitting that or used to hit it; you saw how her hair was messy and he was sweating when the door opened, right?” Mohammad stresses the nonsense to Antonio.

“I wasn't paying attention like that. Yo, that dude just told me he knows my brother,” Antonio changes the subject.

“Oh word? Well, I mean these dudes are from the same neighborhoods we’re from. That’s nothing rare...”

“Yeah…I guess. You ready for lockout? It’s 4:30pm,” he reminds him, unsure of how he’s going to pull this off.

“Yeah, um, give it another 5 minutes. Lock out 8 cell. He does chow and I want him to clean the food pantry before the Captain gets here,” Mohammad tries to finagle a thought.

Antonio turns the knob and cell 8 opens. Inmate Dice peeks out, wiping the cold out his eye and signals a thumbs up.

"Hurry up, man, it's almost lockout time!"

Mohammad unlocks the slop sink closet and steps inside as much as he can. He digs into his pocket and retrieves the pack of cigarettes he has for Dice, throwing them in the sink. He's so sloppy, Antonio watches the whole ordeal. Dice walks out towards to the A-station.

"What's good, Sanchez?" Dice approaches the A-station with cockiness.

"Wow. This shit just keeps getting more and more bugged out," Antonio shakes his head, mumbling to himself.

CO Garçon grabs a few things from the vending machine after getting stuck with 8 hours of mandatory overtime. She's furious and working the B-officer post in the Protective Custody housing area known for housing rapists, child molesters, and inmates who have gang affiliated problems that are hiding from the general population. CO Jones walks in and places his lunch inside the refrigerator and then walks to the vending machine standing to her side.

"What's going on, G? You doing a double, huh?" Jones stands, deciding what snack to purchase.

"Yeah, these mothafuckas got me…6 Upper at that! It's cool though, I'm out at 11pm on the dot. I can still go out to the club. What's going on with you, Mr. Ladies' Man?"

He laughs, "I think I'm trying to lay off the ladies for a while. I need a woman with a good head on her shoulders, these young chicks are outta their minds."

"I hear that. You sound like you need to unwind. Me and my girls have a section tonight, pull up. I'll text you prior to leaving. You let me know, cool?"

"I'm all the way down. I hit my overtime cap this week anyway so I'll see you there," Jones promises.

They both part ways and CO Garçon walks to the very end of the corridor where the Protective Custody Unit is located. It's isolated on purpose to prevent any contact from the general population. Walking up the stairs, she bangs the door to get inside. The A-officer comes to open the door and is alone while the inmates remain locked in.

"Hey, what's going on?" the random correction officer greets.

"Chillin. House was quiet?" Ms. G questions.

“Yeah, for the most part. Only issue was Inmate Jackson and Inmate Hanes. I'm pretty sure you know Jackson, right? He just got out the Box.”

“Oh, God, yes of course. He’s infamous. Why are they beefing?”

“Well, Hanes just came to the house this morning. He was all over the paper and the inmates know who he is. Jackson wants to be an anti-rapist hero so he’s been taunting him all morning, calling him names and gestures, and also threatening his life. The Captain knows about it. They might move Hanes to the A- side to avoid Jackson.

“Okay, copy. I’ll let the A-officer know once they arrive. Let me in on the B-side so I can do this count then go talk to Jackson,” she tells him. She rather get some insight and set the tone before letting anyone out, especially Jackson.

She does her count and then proceeds to the A-side. Jackson is already at his door peeking through the crack to see who the officer is. They speak through the Plexiglas of his cell.

“Hi, Ms.G. You here with us today?” Jackson greets her in a low voice.

"Yes, I am. You just got out the Box and you causing issues already they told me."

"Nah, far from it. This dude is a creep, man. He's the one who was trying to rape women in Central Park. When you see him, you'll feel how awkward that mothafucka is. Anyway, I'm going to chill since you here. I was going to set his whole cell on fire, for real!" he assures her.

"I hear that. Listen, we going to have a chill one. I'll be on the floor, so you can keep me company, cool?"

"Cool, cool, it's a date," he smiles.

She continues her count and walks to let the officer she just relieved out, and as she does so her partner for the evening is none other than CO Johnson who strolls up the flight of stairs out of breath but as fabulous as ever.

"Hey, Missy! You working with me today?" she questions Ms. G.

"I'm here. I know you have some good Jamaican food with you today, I can smell it!" she giggles.

"You know I do! The officer just told me the situation, so let's keep an eye on the new guy. I'm not worried about Jackson, he's always a sweetheart with me," she affirms.

“Yes, same here,” Garçon agrees.

Loud banging and yelling begins from a cell on the side Garçon just left.

“What the fuck is that?” she walks over to the cell, “What’s the problem, sir? Stop banging.”

Inmate Hanes, 6’3 African male with bulging eyes, appears at the cell door with no shirt on, and the horrid smell of funk and dirty mop water reeks from his wall. Inmate Hanes has not showered in over 6 days.

“I can’t live here!” he yells in a strong accent.

“Okay, first, let’s lower your tone. I'm right here, no need to yell,” she demands.

He’s furious, “If you don’t move me, it’s going to be a problem. Stop playing with me!”

“We’ll see about that,” Garçon laughs, indicating that she’s not worried.

She walks away and Inmate Jackson watches her from his cell. It’s lockout time and CO Johnson begins to press the knobs one by one and the inmates slowly walk out. Garçon stands firm watching Hanes walk out and is on point. He walks right by her into the dayroom and sits down among the older inmates. He watches TV as if nothing is wrong. Inmate Jackson gives her a head nod insinuating that he's got her back. Captain Mitchell walks in to the housing area and checks in.

"Hello, ladies. How's everyone?" the captain questions her staff.

"We're good, getting the house ready for chow. I have a total count of 11 on each side so it should be quick," Johnson states.

"Garçon, you on a double, right?"

"Yes ma'am. Tired, but I'll be alright."

"Any issues?" Captain Mitchell looks at them both, stopping her pen while filling in the log book entry.

Inmate Hanes walks slowly over to the bubble to try to speak with Captain Mitchell regarding his issue. He interjects.

"Excuse me, Captain, can I speak to you please?" he stops where the inmate phones are located, disregarding the other inmate's privacy.

"Did you speak to my officer prior to speaking to me?" she questions, making sure inmates follow the chain of command.

"She didn't want to hear me out, ma'am," he pleads to her.

“Wait! What? All you did was scream and bang on your cell door. You never told me anything aside from ‘I can’t live here,’” Garçon mocks his heavy accent.

“Why can’t you live here, Mr. Hanes?”

“Dudes want to come at me because I been in the newspaper for shit I didn’t do!”

“You’re in Protective Custody, this is technically the only place you can be without an issue,” she reminds him, “Let me call the movement office and see what your situation is and I’ll call back. If it’s a go, I’ll get you transferred, ok?”

She knows deep down that movement is not going to move him just because he claims he “can’t live here.” If it was that easy, they’d get called at least 100 times. Most inmates play that game because there are not enough drugs in the house or they feel unsafe at the moment due to their friends not being present. People do better with numbers.

“Yes ma’am,” he agrees.

Garçon rolls her eyes, puts her back against the wall, and writes into her log book. Inmate Jackson walks close by and acts as if he’s about to get on the phone.

Hanes turns his head slowly and looks at Garçon, “I’m no fucking rapist either! And if I was one, I wouldn't stick my dick in your hood rat ass if you paid me!”

Garçon drops her log book to the floor, "Eat a dick! You nasty, old, good for nothing, thirsty, disgusting, rapist bitch! That's all you are is a bitch!

"I can't live here!" she mimics him in his voice. "You fucking clown," she shouts directly in his direction.

She gets in his face and he stands firm, not saying a word, but his eyes pierce right through her. Inmate Jackson watches and is ready to pounce on him the second he makes a wrong move.

"Hey! That's enough! Listen! Hanes, I'm moving you to the A-side until I hear from the movement office to transfer you to another Protective Custody housing area in another building. For now, go grab your property from your cell and you'll go to the A-side, 19 cell, okay?" Captain Mitchell shouts.

He stares at Garçon and slowly steps back, "Yes ma'am, thank you!"

Antonio walks into the staff kitchen holding his water bottle and goes straight to the vending machine. It's practically empty, so he just grabs a seat and positions it towards the TV where other officers are enjoying the NBA finals. CO Johnson walks in a few seconds after and notices Antonio seated alone.

She grabs the chair and sits next to him, “Hey, honey bun! How you feeling? How you like it so far? You do remember me, right? From ya first night with ya cousin?”

“Oh, hey! Yes, of course I remember you, Ms. J. How you feeling?”

“I’m okay, my love. How’s your cousin doing? Word around here is that after her fainting incident she’s getting transferred and moving to headquarters. Is that true?” Johnson questions.

“I’m not 100% on that one, but if she does then she’ll have an easy career. Not having to deal with inmates would be a gift,” Antonio answers.

“I’m hoping it is true. She deserves it. A lot of people here talk behind her back saying that she is an inmate lover and all that nonsense, but what they don’t realize is that she’s a human before anything and she knows how to talk to these guys and they respect her for that. When she first started, all the inmates respected her and listened to her every word, and let me tell you, that’s earned not given.”

“Yeah, she’s one of a kind.”

There is a voice on the radio, "10-11! 10-11! IN PROGRESS! ALL AVAILABLE STAFF REPORT TO THE STAGING AREA!"

The alarm rings inside the staff kitchen along with the siren lights located right above the 72-inch flat screen TV showing the basketball game. Officers drop their food on the table, pissed off that the game's almost over and now they have to run to the staging area to respond to the alarm.

Antonio drops his water bottle and rushes out. CO Johnson barely flinches and remains seated. She feels she's responded to enough alarms in her career, so she allows the new and more youthful officers to do so.

He gets to the staging area and dawns on the riot gear. Vest first and helmet second, and another officer hands batons. All the Captains and Assistant Deputy Wardens make their way towards the central control office. Another officer comes and grabs the camera. Captain Davis places his vest and helmet on and sees the rookie officer, Antonio, was the first to be fully ready.

He leans over to him and talks through his helmet, "This your first time responding?"

"Yes sir!" Antonio answers.

“Let’s wait for the Warden’s instructions. Follow directly behind me, copy?”

“Yes sir!”

Antonio is nervous. He’s not shaking, but adrenaline is flowing through his veins. Not knowing where or what the alarm might consist of, he wants to make a good impression with the staff. Warden Saunders stands by with the radio in hand, communicating with the central control about what set off the alarm.

The voice on the radio answers, “Assault on staff, 6 Upper! Proceed with the first wave.”

“That’s us, Sanchez, come on!”

Davis leads the first wave of officers through the corridor. A total of four officers, including Antonio, march directly behind the Captain, clutching their wooden batons in hand just like they were taught in the academy. Antonio looks back and doesn't recognize any of the three officers behind him. They run up the stairs and the door is opened by the meal relief officer who had just relieved CO Johnson for her break.

They rush in and see Inmate Hanes handcuffed and sporting a bloody nose and lip and swollen eye, lying on his stomach directly in front of the A-station. CO Garçon, out of breath, has her flashlight in hand.

"Garçon, are you okay!?" Davis questions.

She's out of breath, "I'm good! This piece of shit went to swing on me when he was let out to transfer from the B-side to the A-side. He tried to swing and grab me to pin me up against the wall! I pushed him away and I couldn't grab my pepper spray, so I took out my flashlight and defended myself!" she huffs.

"That's fucking bullshit, Captain! She and another inmate jumped me, man! She's lying! I had my property door opened and I got hit with the flashlight on my eye then another inmate two pieced me, Captain! She lying!" he pleads.

The response team stands by and picks Inmate Hanes up from the ground. Captain Davis grabs his radio and calls central control.

Captain Davis gets on the radio, "Please be advised, incident under control, stand by for more information."

Antonio lifts the plastic guard covering his face for some fresh air. He steps over to Garçon.

"G, what's good? Seems like you handled this pretty well, I ran over here to help, but you won already!" Antonio says.

"I told you I don't play with these bozos. I'm from Brooklyn! I've fought guys twice his size!" Garçon assures this was something light.

The team escorts Inmate Hanes out.

"Garçon, when you get a chance, I need an incident report, injury report, and infraction, copy?" Captain Davis demands from her.

"Copy!"

"Matter of fact, Sanchez dawn your equipment and hand it to the meal relief officer. You're taking over the A-station until Johnson gets back and then I want you to get on the A-side. I want two officers on the floor here. I'll have the meal relief officer take care of your post in 5 main, copy?"

Antonio stands taking in what the Captain just asked of him, "Copy…sir."

"Damn, Captain, 5 main?" the meal relief officer is confused.

"I don't think I stuttered, did I?" Captain Davis is firm.

Everyone exits the housing area except Antonio and Garçon. They enter the bubble after Antonio hands over the riot gear, vest, and helmet.

"Bastard tried to get loud with me and threaten me, he must be crazy!" she continues to state.

"I see that flashlight came in handy! Why did he keep saying he got jumped?" Antonio jokes.

"Well, once he got too close I felt like he wanted to brush up on me on his way out the door, so I hit him with it then Jackson from the A-side came and clocked him twice. He fell and we went to work on him. Listen, a lot of these inmates will have your back. Jackson knew that if the door closed and it was just me and that guy in front of the bubble, he could've taken advantage of me and who knows where this could've gone!"

"Oh shit! But the meal relief officer should've helped you, no?" Antonio asks.

"Sanchez, let me tell you something, a lot of these officers have, STD, SCARED TO DEATH! They don't want no parts in the physical action, and I'm all about it. That officer remained in the bubble and just kept yelling 'Stop!' I didn't mention it to the captain, but trust me, he knows. Captain Davis is not stupid, that's why he made him go to your housing area and not remain here. He knows that for not assisting me, I was going to verbally violate him," Garçon expresses herself.

Antonio grins and nods in agreement, "You can definitely hold your own!"

"Also, be mindful, you see how you were the first response team and you're brand new staff. They see you're not scared to get your hands dirty, not that you should, but they see you're prepared for it. Keep that shit up, you'll gain great respect here, believe that!" Garçon gets up and looks towards the B-side.

"Jackson!" Garçon shouts.

Jackson walks out the shower, perfectly calm, as if nothing occurred, "What's going on, Ms. G?"

"Here," she hands him a chocolate bar and two bags of chips through the gate slot inside the A-station.

He extends his arm grabbing both.

"When I go to lunch in a few, I have some Rasta Pasta with chicken and shrimp. I'm going to save you some, okay?"

"Okay, Ms. G, thank you!" he walks away into the dayroom to enjoy his snacks.

"You not afraid the other inmates saw that you gave him outside food?" Antonio asks.

"It's just chips, Sanchez. Officers here give sexual favors to guys, you think anyone going to say shit?

Negative, these inmates are human, too. Be human to them," she assures.

"Yeah, no definitely, totally agree."

Upstairs at the visitor's floor, CO Jones allows the bus of visitors to enter the door and begins the property search. The last person to get off the bus is Mya, dressed in baggy clothing. They lock eyes. He allows everyone in front of her to walk up the ramp and closes the door in her face, then cracks it slowly.

"Give me a minute, miss, only 12 at a time," Jones states.

Mya rolls her eyes as he closes the door again. A few seconds later, he opens.

"Any cell phones, contraband, or weapons on your person? You're allowed to discard one last time in the amnesty box located to your left without any questioning," Jones continues.

"I'm clear of any of that, sir."

He lets her in. She clears the metal detector and places her bag through the conveyer belt while another visitor officer clears her to move forward. Jones tries to pay her little mind as she is directed to place her belongings into the visitor lockers. Jones sits behind his desk, watching her every move. She puts away her purse and proceeds upstairs. He trails behind her.

"Excuse me, miss, what's the last name of the inmate you're here to visit?" Jones questions. He asks as if he's unsure or has never seen here.

"Danny Rios, sir" Mya answers with attitude.

Jones challenges, "Rios? Um, okay, got it!"

She walks around the tables and is told by another officer where to sit. She knows this routine just as well as they do and sits casually, keeping both hands visible for the officers. CO Jones starts to wonder what her objective is, knowing her boyfriend is restricted from having a visit unless it's through a glass. Remembering that he was instructed to let the Captain know of her arrival, to detain her, he's hesitant. She might be pregnant, she might expose him for sleeping with her, she might make it known that she is a minor. The visitors come in and he sees the inmate with whom she's here to check in.

He walks to him, "Rios, right!?"

Flacko looks confused, "Yeah, what's up?"

"You see your visitor?"

"She's right there with the green sweater," Flacko points.

"Okay, go sit down. I'm watching ya," Jones warns.

Flacko looks at him with disgust. Jones is savvy to who is involved in what gang. He knows Shorty, Mya's boyfriend, and Flacko are both Latin King. To him, it's obvious what's about to transpire. To others, it's just a regular visit. They hug and sit down.

"What's good? How you feeling?" Flacko asks.

"I'm okay. What's up with Shorty? How much time until he gets his phone privileges back? I really need to speak to him, it's urgent."

"You know that's like my brother in here, whatever you need, tell me. Tell me here and I'll make sure he gets word. Other than that, how we doing this? That CO is on our body right now," Flacko tells her to make her feel comfortable.

"Don't worry about him, he knows what's up. I have that bozo wrapped around my finger," she expresses with confidence.

Flacko glances in his direction and smiles, "Here, move a little closer to me. Kiss me," he guides her.

She's hesitant, so Flacko does exactly that. CO Jones speed walks to them.

"Yo! No kissing during the visit unless it's at the end. This is a warning to both of ya," Jones preaches.

"Sorry, CO. I haven't seen my baby in a few weeks, I apologize."

Jones grills Mya, obviously disturbed, as he walks away from them. Mya slips a balloon from her mouth into Flacko's hands and Flacko quickly pops it in his mouth and swallows it whole. The visit continues. Jones, among other officers, walks the visitor floor making sure everyone's following rules and regulations. Jones constantly makes eye contact with Mya but does nothing.

Back by the main entrance, alongside the control room, Calbo walks into a room shackled and escorted by an officer who opens the door to Calbo's lawyer, Mark Gold. Mark is a Caucasian man with a pony tail, known for an extraordinary record in the courts. He's been getting guys way less prison time than demanded by his fellow prosecutors. He stands up from the desk to shake Calbo's hand. The officer steps out and Calbo sits directly across from his lawyer, who has a stack of folders and paperwork on the desk.

"Did you get injured in the riot?" Gold asks, already aware.

"Nothing crazy, minor burn on my back and neck from hot water."

"That whole shit made the news, man. The President of the Union was interviewed and everything. I'm pretty sure they plan on firing the probationary officer who pressed the button that opened both sides, poor girl. Well, anyway, like every visit we have in-person, good news and bad news," Gold affirms.

"They still talking 15 years?" Calbo questions sternly.

"100%! This is your third felony, Arroyo, yes. Your priors are drug cases and yes, they are non-violent, but this is an attempted murder. You're not very liked by the Manhattan District Attorney's office like you once were. They gave you not one but two golden tickets for the drug stuff," Gold continues.

"I know, I know. Have they reached out to you?"

"Well, that's why I am here, Mr."

Calbo jokes, "Well, shit, I don't have anyone else to give them. The dope boys and big ballers from my hood received football numbers with all the information I gave them. Nobody's left."

"They are aware of that, but they do want to inquire about activity that occurs here, on Rikers."

"Activity here? What, like gang shit?" he's confused.

"That...maybe drugs that come in here, corrupt correction officers who bring them. They had a meeting with DOI, Department of Investigation and the Inspector General's office, they want to crack down on correction officers doing the wrong thing, and your name came up. The only reason it came up is because you, as an inmate, are in the midst of it all. You're basically their potential inside man."

"So they just want me to snitch on officers bringing in tobacco or weed and shit and then what, they cutting my time?" Calbo questions.

"Well, I'm pretty sure they want the juicy stuff. COs giving a guy a pack of Newport isn't front page news. They want to make a statement. The Mayor's office and the Internal Affairs Bureau are under scrutiny and they're thirsty for a trophy. Are you interested?"

Calbo pauses and looks down at his shackled wrists then makes sturdy eye contact for about 10 seconds, "I'm down, just get me more details. I think I could set something up, but let them know they have to accommodate me if they want the juicy shit."

"I'll have them set up a meeting. Don't be surprised if you randomly get called in the next few days to go to court. They'll bring you through a back door into an office.

I'll be present and you'll get a better understanding of what's needed from you, and we'll negotiate from there. Remember man, time's ticking."

"Copy."

Lawyer Gold gathers his folders and walks out. Calbo sits still with his eyes closed and inhales deeply. The escort officer opens the door and guides him out back to the Box where he is being held after the riot.

CHAPTER 7

Antonio starts to get his groove and becomes very liked by his peers, the inmates, and the officers equally. His body language is welcoming, he's learned the thin line of being a people person, lending his ear, and having an open door policy, but also enforcing rules and regulations. He keeps getting assigned the high classification housing areas because he's known amongst his superiors to hold his own. Word gets around that he has a brother who's currently incarcerated on the Island, and out of the respect and reputation that Diego holds, inmates throughout the building salute him. His cousin, Julissa, is also well respected and her romance with Dollar is the cherry on top. Dollar tells his peers to respect Antonio and not give him a hard time. Antonio becomes rookie of the year in a sense, but he doesn't take advantage. He remains humble and opens his heart to all, regardless of what side they're on. He sits patiently in the A-station bubble alongside CO Garçon; they joke and laugh at a video they just watched on her phone.

"That's crazy! Oh, man, I needed that laugh. Be careful bringing in your phone, they're cracking down on people and taking away vacation days if you get caught with one," Antonio reminds her.

"I know, they mentioned it at roll call. I need my phone on me though. 8-16 hours with no outside entertainment has me feeling like I'm doing time myself. Social media is my outlet for real," Garçon jokes.

"I agree. After today, I'm off for six days. I'm going to Miami for Labor Day, much needed."

"Really! So am I. I leave Saturday. Let's link out there!" she flirts.

"Yes definitely! I don't usually chill with co-workers, but we click on a whole other level," he admits to her.

"I feel the same way!" Garçon blushes.

She gets up and yells "ON THE LOCKOUT UGLY BOYS!" She turns the knobs of all the occupied cells, letting the inmates out one by one. They pass the A-station and acknowledge the COs with a peace sign or head nod, grabbing the phones and into the dayroom area. Killah, Ms. Garçon's "boo," walks to the bubble.

"Sanchez, what's up, bro? How you feeling?" Killah greets.

"I'm good, man. You saw your man Kobe last night!?" Antonio sparks conversation.

"I did, but they forced us to lock in because it was after 11 and they went into overtime twice."

"Damn, that's whack. I hope they win tonight though."

"Yeah, bro, hope so. Hi, Ms. G. How you feeling?" Killah turns his attention to CO Garçon.

"I'm fine, sir. Please go to the pantry area and get the food ready. I want to get chow out the way."

Killah looks at her and shakes his head, "Yo, Sanchez, when you get a chance, pull up, I want to holla at you about something. You can let your friend, Ms. G, know later, but I rather tell you first."

"I got you, bro," Antonio assures him.

Garçon buzzes Antonio onto the housing area floor and he walks into the pantry area with Killah.

"What's good?" Antonio inquires.

"Your homeboy that you work with randomly here…Mohammad."

"Yeah, Mo! What's up?" Antonio questions.

"He's making the house hot, man, bringing in shit to some cat in here. I'm not going to sugarcoat shit, I been getting high more than usually because of it. He bringing in some fire, but he's too sloppy, and I know the search team is aware of it because when you or Ms. G not working, this house reeks of it. Mohammad is cool, he's a weirdo, but a cool one. I don't want him or any of you guys to go under the radar, feel me? Especially since you work alongside one another, I know you don't be with that."

"Oh, wow. I appreciate you telling me. I'm gonna holla at him, but trust me, I won't mention you," Antonio seems surprised.

"Yeah, definitely, you already know," Killah assures.

Killah continues setting up the food from the cart into the pantry and begins serving chow to the inmates in the housing area. Antonio exits out the door as if nothing was said.

Flacko returns from the visitor floor after being stripped search and successfully getting the drugs from Mya. As he walks the corridor back to his dorm, he realizes he can go straight to work if the officer in the barbershop allows him. He gets to the door and knocks. The barbershop CO is CO Mohammad. Mohammad cracks the door.

"What's going on? Who you?" Mohammed asks.

"I work here, CO. I just left the visitor floor, but I want to work before going back to my housing area," Flacko says.

Not convinced, Mohammad continues to question him, "Um, what house are you in and what's your last name?"

"Rios. Dorm 12, Danny Rios."

Mohammad closes the door in his face and checks the log books to verify that Flacko is an actual barber. He picks up the phone and calls dorm 12 to ask if letting him come straight to work form the visitor floor is allowed. He gets the okay and hangs up. Walking back to the door, he gives him the thumbs up.

"Ok, man, you good. The CO told me to tell you next time, stop by the dorm first," Mohammad's tone falls back.

"Oh ok, thank you. How you feeling? You here all day or are you just doing the lunch relief?" Flacko makes small talk. He steps in and greets the other two barbers cleaning their clippers and setting up for the upcoming housing area to come.

"I'm just here for the day. Your boss, the steady officer, called out," he expresses.

"Ok, that's cool. What house is coming in right now?"

"I believe it's 5 main, only the A- side today," he affirms.

As Flacko sets up at his station, Antonio, who's the escort officer, knocks with 6 inmates lined up holding the haircut vouchers for which they paid $2 at commissary.

"What's good, Mo? I was just talking about you, man. You ready for these guys?" Antonio questions.

Mohammad smiles a little, "Oh, for real? Good or bad talk?"

"That's debatable. Let these guys in so we can chop it up," Antonio tells him.

Mohammed collects the inmates' vouchers and checks if the IDs match. The very last inmate is Dice who does not have a voucher. Haircut vouchers are purchased at commissary for $2. For inmates with no money on their books and upcoming court dates, the department allows a free haircut.

"Where's your voucher, sir?" Mohammad questions.

"Nah, man. I misplaced it during a search the other day. The team threw away all my property, but I'm telling you I had it. Ask Sanchez, he'll vouch for me," he pleads.

Antonio is visibly uneasy, "Yeah, man, he's good. This one's on me."

They walk in and Dice begins to talk to Flacko in Spanish, and sits in his barber chair. CO Mohammad gives Dice a head nod and pulls out a chair for Antonio to sit alongside him at the desk. The inmates police themselves on who goes next or what barber they choose, which normally is assigned. Mohammad always gave the "oh, he's cool and lets you do whatever CO" so they know it's a free for all. Antonio heads into the officer bathroom to check his cellphone that he knows he shouldn't have, but it's on constant watch after his mother's boyfriend has been on the run from the domestic violence incident. He's always checking in on her and her whereabouts.

He sees a recent text and 2 missed calls from her. He texts her back, "Mom, I'm working and can't call you. You ok?"

"Yes papa! Good news, they arrested Roberto! I can finally rest. He was arraigned this morning and they didn't give him bail because he was on the run. He might go to Rikers, please be careful. Don't tell Diego or your cousin! I don't want them doing anything or getting themselves involved."

Nervously Antonio texts back, "Ok, ma, that is good news. YOU be careful. The police might want you to come in for more questioning. Let them know you want me to be present, if they need you to come in, okay? In case you don't understand something, I want to be there!"

He puts his phone away, flushes the toilet, and washes his hands. He takes a look in the mirror and washes his face. He needs to keep composure and hurry home to comfort her. As he opens the door, he notices Mohammad standing behind Flacko cutting Dice's hair. Antonio calls him over.

"Yo, once my inmates are done, I'll take them back to the housing area. I'm gonna come back and chop it up with you about some shit, and I'm going to need you to keep it real."

Mohammad gives a blank stare of defeat, "Yeah man, definitely. This is actually the last house I have before the count, so we'll be here alone. Do you have to do the 3pm search?" Mohammad questions.

"I do, but I'll fall back. I don't think Captain Davis will care if I miss out," Antonio reverts. He pauses. "Listen, Mo, my family always used to tell me, 'If you going to do something wrong, make sure you do it right,'" Antonio quotes.

There's an awkward silence, Antonio closes the door and steps out, walking towards the central control room to retrieve another battery for his radio. Passing the intake area, he sees the inmates in the holding pens located in the corridor. He glances over and notices his mother's ex- boyfriend, Roberto. What a crazy coincidence…Roberto is pacing back and forth, but he doesn't realize it's Antonio walking right by him. Antonio speed walks in an attempt to avoid any conversation. He can't catch a break. His anxiety and stress become so overwhelming; he is relieved he doesn't have to come into work tomorrow.

Newly suspended CO Tiffany Thompson sits on a park bench while her 3-year-old daughter eats an ice cream cone next to her. She's been suspended without pay and may possibly lose her job due to the incidents that escalated in her house after her nervous negligence. Her phone rings and it's Union President Simmons.

"Sister Thompson, I hope all is well and you're keeping faith. We have not stopped in our fight to get you off your current suspension. The department is trying to have you resign respectfully due to you still being a probationary officer. My argument towards that is, well, why isn't the other officer being reprimanded? He was also on probation, but the underlying factor is his dad is a retired warden who knows everyone and they're trying to justify the fact that you're the one who had access to the doors opening because you were in the A-station. Regardless, it's my duty to fight till the very end for you! It's not going to be easy. This officer is also white. We all wear blue, but at the end of the day, the segregation still exists no matter what side you're on," Simmons loudly explains over the phone.

"Yes, sir, please. I don't want to lose my job. This is more than a job, it's my career. I'm a single mother. I just moved out of my parents' house, I can't afford to lose this," she pleads softly.

"I'm giving it my all, sis! My team and I, trust me! I will keep you posted and see what the department's final decision will be by the end of this week. Rikers has been under extreme scrutiny with the gang violence. My officers are getting hurt at an all-time high due to the use of force, suicides, and overall corruption, so they're trying to come down hard on anyone and everyone, including myself.

They despise me because I am a minority and I fight for us. They want me out, too!" Simmons continues.

"Thank you so much, sir! I appreciate you and hope we can come to something, even if I lose my vacation days, but please, I need to keep my job," her voice begins to crack.

"We fighting, sis! Speak to you soon!"

They hang up and she sheds a light tear.

Antonio walks back towards the barbershop to escort his inmates who are done getting their haircuts. CO Mohammad has them come out to the corridor and line up against the gate, he locks the door.

"Fellas, on the noise, two-line formation!" Mohammad shouts.

"Oh, shit, Mo! You got this down pat, huh?" Antonio is surprised by his stern voice.

"These guys know me. I'm cool, just reciprocate and work with me," he states.

The inmates line up quietly and prepare to walk to their housing area. Mohammad leads the front and Antonio stays behind. They get to the housing area and yell "5 MAIN!" CO Garçon walks out the A-station and opens the gate.

"That's all of them, Sanchez?" she asks.

"That's all of them. I'll be back after the lockout. If you need me, have central control
radio me."

CO Garçon gives CO Mohammad a nasty up and down look, "Be mindful with the company you keep, Sanchez!" she throws out the comment in hopes of making Mohammad feel uncomfortable.

Antonio and Mohammad walk off towards the staff kitchen and head outside to the smoking area. Mohammad lights a cigarette and offers him one. Surprisingly, he takes it. He's got some much going on, he's stressing out. Since no one's around, they can openly have the conversation.

"So, what's up, man? What exactly did you need to ask or put me on to? You had me thinking about that whole 'if you're going to do something wrong, make sure you do it right' shit," Mohammad asks him, particularly nervous.

Antonio looks around, "If I ask you something, you going to keep it real? No sugarcoating nothing, right?" he whispers.

"Always, man, just ask. We too cool to be keeping secrets, bro!" he assures him.

“You bringing in shit for these cats, man? It’s a yes or no question, don’t wiggle around it, bro,” Antonio’s tone demands Mohammad to tell him the truth.

Mohammad stares at Antonio dead in his face and nods yes.

“Hear me out, bro. It all started after I got splashed with urine by that inmate, you remember, right?” he pleaded to only justify his actions.

“Yes, I do. You wanted to kill that guy after that,” Antonio recalls.

“Right! Well, I spoke to this other inmate after and he told me he can handle that for me because he knows I’m cool and that wasn’t right.”

“So, you gave him drugs to handle your dirty work?” he continues to investigate.

“No! Not drugs, just a few loose cigarettes, nothing major. After a while of always working in that housing area, we started talking about me bringing in more cigs and even a little weed here and there. Dude offered me $700 for some weed and a few packs of Newport’s, and aside form you being my boy, the main reason I’m telling you this is because he told me he’s your brother’s best friend!”

Antonio ponders, “Wait! You talking about Dice?”

"Yeah, man. I'm not proud of this shit, but I been fucked up. These checks aren't what they're cracked up to be. I was backed up on rent, my girl just found out she's pregnant, I have school debt through the roof. It's not going to be forever. I'm going to fuck around a few more times and I'm done!"

"Just be mindful. In my eyes, it's not worth it, but I'm not judging you. What did he say about my brother though?" Antonio inquires.

"Nothing much, just he knows you," he shrugs.

"Listen, I'm going to join the 3pm search. I still have time to make it, and I don't want to get written up. Just please be careful and don't be sloppy, man. These cats see everything and they talk a lot, and if I know about it, I'm pretty sure others do, too," he warns. Antonio would hate to see someone bothered.

They give each other a handshake and brotherly hug. Antonio walks out and heads to the 3pm institutional search. When he arrives to 7 main, where the search is almost over, Captain Davis comes out and stops Antonio in his tracks.

"Too busy to join us, Sanchez?" Davis states under his breath.

"No sir, I was escorting the guys from the barbershop back to their housing area."

"That's a reasonable excuse. Do me a favor, since you don't mind escorting, take this inmate with his property to dorm 10. The movement office lowered his classification. Thank you."

The inmate walks out and it's Calbo. Calbo doesn't have on any cuffs and throws his property bag over his shoulders.

"Captain Davis, thank you!" Calbo exclaims.

"No problem. I'll come check in on you later today," Davis reminds him.

Calbo gives Antonio a head nod and they walk up the stairs, taking the long way to the other side of the building. As soon as they cut the corner, Calbo looks to see if anyone is in ear shot.

"Yo CO, personal question. You Diego's little brother, right?" Calbo questions.

Antonio retracts, "Excuse me? Listen, man, I'm not here for that."

"Diego and I been in wars together here. That's my guy. Respectfully, that's my brother, too, I'm just telling you what it is."

"Ok, that's good for you. Not my business, man," he answers as if he's careless about the whole situation.

Calbo stops and drops his bag, "I'm tired. Give me a second to catch my breath, please. My bag is super heavy."

Antonio waits. Calbo gathers his bag again and they continue to walk. With no one in the corridors due to the institutional count, Calbo takes advantage and keeps the conversation going.

"You cool with Dollar, too, right? He told me to tell you he sends his love. He was in the Box with me."

Antonio's uneasy, "Yeah, I know Dollar. He's cool or whatever."

"He told me to holla at you, that you might be interested," he whispers.

Antonio is clearly offended, "Interested in what?"

"Come on, Sanchez, getting this money, man. What else?"

"Nah, man, sorry. That's not my sport. I make way too much money here to mess that up."

"You haven't even heard my offer, brother," Calbo jokes.

Antonio stops walking in anger; he looks at Calbo in disgust, "I don't care about your offer. I don't need it. I wouldn't risk my job bringing you and or anyone here anything!"

"I respect that, but I wasn't asking you to bring me anything. Listen to what I gotta say and you sit on it. You won't do outside security?" he fronts.

"Outside security?" he ponders.

They arrive to the dorm and before Antonio knocks on the door for the officer to let Calbo in, there's an awkward silence.

"Give it a thought, bro. A quick $1,000 a night, a few days out the week, will benefit you and help my company while I'm stuck in here fighting my case. It's a win, win!" he continues to swindle.

Antonio becomes dismissive, "Yeah, ok, have a good one. DORM 10!"

He bangs the door and the officer comes and lets Calbo in. Antonio hands over his floor card and walks out. He shakes his head and heads back to 1 main to chill with Garçon in the A-station. A few hours go by and it's almost time for Antonio to leave. He's desperate to go to see his mother and he promised his younger sister he'd be home tonight to watch a movie.

His radio sounds, "Sanchez, Officer Sanchez, landline central control room!"

He looks at Garçon and gets up from his seat to dial.

He answers the phone, “Sanchez.”

“Sanchez, you’re stuck tonight! 9pm-5am! Overnight sanitation post, I’m giving you something easy!” Captain Davis tells him, acting as if he threw him a bone.

“I can’t today, Capt.!” Antonio pleads.

“You want a write up for being AWOL or you want to do this easy post and get it over with? Better yet take this today and I’ll pardon you the next time, I promise,” the Captain tries to negotiate.

“Damn, ok, fine. Can you tell me who the workers are?” he asks.

“They’re all in dorm 10. The officer has the list! Thank you!” Captain Davis hangs up on him.

“Damn, stuck?” Garçon looks at him already knowing the answer.

“Yeah, I fucking hate this shit. I had so much to do at home,” Antonio sucks his teeth, frustrated.

Mohammad waits patiently, but very nervously. He fidgets around, parked up at the dead end. His phone rings and the screen says “Flacko’s Girl.” He answers.

“Hey, I’m outside your building. I’m headed to your car,” a young woman’s voice sounds.

The door opens, and it's Mya holding a black bag in one hand and a water bottle in the other. She climbs into the passenger seat.

"Hi. Here, the money is in the bag, too, if you need to count it," she states.

He grabs it and throws it in the back seat, all smiles.

"What's the water bottle for?" he spots it in her hand.

"It's Vodka. He told me to bring this to you, too," she tells him as if it's something regular.

"Wow! I don't know about this, that's a little too much," he looks at it up and down, checking the contents.

"Well, I don't know, you guys deal with that. I'm just here to hand it to you and that's all I'm doing," she states while texting on her phone and scrolling through her social media.

"Ok, um, I'll see what I can do. How much cash was in the bag?"

"$700 cash, 8 pouches, and some weed, but I packed it good. It doesn't smell, it's well wrapped. Okay, bye," she gathers herself.

She walks out and slams the door. Mohammed opens the water bottle and smells the content inside. He scratches his nose at how strong it is. He puts it aside and drives off.

Making his way to dorm 10, Antonio gets buzzed in. CO Johnson finishes her count and opens the A-station door for him. She had just left the staff bathroom where she took a small swig out her thermo-bottle of Vodka and orange juice.

"Hi, Sanchez, how you feeling? How's your cousin?"

"She's doing better. I believe she's out the jails for good and doing administration work at headquarters starting next week," he informs her, noticing she's a little off.

"Good for her! You here to pick up the PM sanitation guy? He just got here, it's weird how the Captain wanted him to have that job, but that's not my business."

"What bed is he in? What's his last name?" Antonio asks, but deep down he remembers exactly where he went.

"I believe he's 33 bed on the B- side, Arroyo. I've seen him before. He's been around for a while, quiet and respectful. Let me tell him to get ready," Johnson gets on the house loudspeaker, "Arroyo! 33 bed Arroyo! PM sanitation, your officer's here."

Inmate Calbo is at the door in seconds, Johnson buzzes him out.

"Oh shit, you got stuck?" Calbo smiles.

"Yeah, unfortunately. How'd you get a job? I just brought you to this dorm?" Antonio asks.

"When they changed my classification, I asked them to give me something quick. I'm not used to sleeping in the dorm because of the open space, so if they were going to put me here, at least give me a job during the night. On top of that, I prevented that riot from escalating more than it did with the Trinitarios and the Crips. Captain Davis, the security team, they all praised me for that, you know. Give to receive, right?"

"So, you got pull basically?"

Calbo grins from ear to ear, "I wouldn't call it pull, I would call it respect. We out?"

"Yeah, we out. Ms. Johnson, I'll bring him back before the 3am count!" he shouts to her.

"I got you, Sanchez, see you!" she gets up to buzz the door and re-enters the staff bathroom to take another swig.

They exit the dorm and take the same stroll towards the back of the kitchen to grab all the supplies needed. Antonio gets a flashback of his first night walking this same corridor with his cousin who he used to brag about potentially working with, then the time her in-house boyfriend and her were joking and flirting and she gave him a package of some sort. He feels conflicted. They get to the supply room. Calbo puts on his headphones and jams to the Spanish radio station, loud enough that Antonio can hear it.

He taps Calbo to get his attention while he grabs the mop.

"Dollar was trying to get me to bring shit in for him. You're not the only one. He's been trying since I met him," Antonio opens.

"That dude don't have no money like that. The dudes under him support him. He's cool and all, but I really do this, Sanchez. Check my paperwork. They seized 1.7 Million in cash from me, bro. You let me know what you're trying to do. I don't come at everyone with this, but you move right. You're not loud, plus you're Dominican. I look out for my people, just like I looked out for your brother that day," Calbo brags.

"Nah, I know. I get it, drop the subject. Let's just get this cleaning over with, ok?" Antonio pushes the conversation away.

"Yeah, yeah. Whenever you ready, but just know this offer going quick. If you don't, I know a few that will, and I'm talking serious money. You haven't even hit top pay, imagine when you do on top of working outside a few days. You'd be making a killing, safely at that. Big crib and car within weeks. Don't believe me, ask around. Check my paperwork, court documents."

"I'm good, man, thank you," Antonio brushes him off.

Calbo puts his headphones on while shaking his head. He closes the closet and they head out to start cleaning.

2 WEEKS LATER

Captain Davis meets with two Department of Investigation detectives. The office walls are almost completely covered with awards of his duty. He's been with the department for over 20 years and has been sanctioned to join DOI for a sting operation they been working on for a few months. He meets with Investigator Allan, a female investigator who has worked alongside the Department of Corrections and the NYPD's internal investigation unit, mostly dealing with illegal drugs and contraband. The other investigator is Ortiz, a Correction Captain who is employed by DOI in a joint task force and is promoting Captain Davis.

"Captain Davis, finally after so many back and forth conference calls, we meet."

"Yes, finally, glad to be a part of this. I guess I wanted to retire with a bang and this seems like the right way," Captain Davis boasts.

"Yeah, man, I love it here. Don't need to work the jails anymore, lots of opportunity for more growth, and the best part is cutting out these bad apples within the department who make our jobs harder and put our safety on the line by bringing these inmates weapons and drugs, putting us in danger," Investigator Ortiz explains.

"Oh, I agree fully. My current building in general goes through contraband phases but these last two years have risen tremendously. I work with the special search team as well and our findings have been bags full. Just the other day we found 18 grams of marijuana on a guy. The way it was packaged, you can tell it was an officer or possibly a civilian. No way that made it through the visit!" Davis breaks it down.

"Yes, I remember seeing the photos for that one. Did the inmate break? He say anything?" he asks.

"Not a word. I told him I'd get his charges dropped and no Box time, even moved to any housing area he pleases, give me something; however, lately I've noticed they only have been giving up each other, no officers," Davis seems defeated.

"What's that inmate you have a familiarity with, the big drug guy that the DEA knows?" Ortiz questions.

"Arroyo? Funny you bring him up. I tried to get him to give me something. He'd rather speak to my gang intelligence unit, but lately he's been comfortable with me. I just moved him out the Box, he told he'd have something for me, but give him some time, whatever that means," Davis tells them.

"You think I should reach out to the DEA office? Special Narcotics, maybe they can call him out for court and I have a sit down with him."

"I can set that up, if he's reliable in the street stuff, I'm pretty sure he can give us something."

"I'll make a few calls today, other than that, welcome to the team, Davis," Ortiz congratulates.

"Thanks, guys. I'm pretty sure I can get something out of him. I been playing him close and he owes me, no charges pending after the riot. I've let other members of the gang he belongs to get away with minor infractions, I got this."

"Beautiful, we'll get together once we get something flowing. I'll contact the DA's office as well!" Ortiz tells.

They all get up and shake hands. Captain Davis logs into his computer and types Calbo's NYSID and docket number. His mug shot and charges come on the screen: **"Attempted Murder: A1 Drug Possession and Conspiracy in the 1st Degree."**

CHAPTER 8

Antonio crosses the bridge, leaving Rikers, and pulls over to park.

Looking through his text messages, he sees a message from Tiffany, “Hey, hope all is well. Doubt I’m getting my job back, but still hopeful. Let’s go out for drinks tomorrow, if you're free!”

He replies, “I’m down. Call you tomorrow to confirm.”

At that moment, Antonio remembers to call the number to inquire about the side gig. He types *67 and then dials the number.

Someone answers in a very heavy accent on the second ring, “Hello. “

“Hello, this is Calbo’s friend,” Antonio slowly responds.

There’s a pause, “Oh, oh. Hello, how are you?” Blanco answers with a heavy Spanish accent.

“I’m good, I’m good. I’m calling about the job,” Antonio inquires.

“I know, I know. What’s your name, man?”

“Um, I’m Juan,” for obvious reasons he doesn't give his real government name.

"Okay, I'm Blanco. You want to not call me private that way we can meet soon, even tonight, if you're able."

"Yeah, I'll call you from my number, just wanted to make sure what it is we're doing, you know?"

"Yes, I understand. Let's meet tomorrow. How about Salsa Restaurant in downtown? 12pm?" Blanco proposes.

"That's a good place, yes. I can be there."

"See you there. Text me your number so I can call you in case I can't make it," Blanco hangs up.

Antonio shoots him a text with his phone number, but gets no reply. He puts his car in drive and heads home with this meeting tomorrow heavy on his mind. He's thinking well, 12pm at a very well-known restaurant in the city doesn't sound too sketchy. He calms himself.

Tiffany exits her car and drops off her sleeping daughter to her waiting mother. She's very dolled up, hair did, long nails, and lots of make-up. Her mom grabs the baby and heads inside. Tiffany returns to her vehicle and drives out for about 20 mins; she parks directly across the street of a strip club. She applies a heavy coat of lip gloss, exits the car, pops the trunk, and she grabs a book bag, her purse, and some 6 inch red leather high heels. Before she started working for the department, Tiffany was a stripper and did this to make ends meet along with attending college. She told herself she'd never return to this life, but after that phone call with the Union President, she needs to pay her bills and provide for her child. She enters and gets her bag checked by security. The place is packed with men and women of all walks. Making her way to the locker room to change, she is greeted by the strip club manager.

"Welcome back, T! Hurry up, we need you on the floor. We've got some big time guys here, and this one dude who just got out of jail is making it rain."

"Cool, thank you," she says not so enthusiastic.

She double checks herself in the mirror and a fellow stripper passes her and hands her a bag containing a white powdered substance. She initially declines but then accepts it, pours some onto the table, and sniffs a whole line before heading onto the stage. The music amplifies and she starts to perform.

THE NEXT DAY

Antonio waits for Blanco at the Colombian restaurant. It's pretty quiet, given the time, but the salsa music playing in the background gives it a lively aesthetic.

After being seated, he orders a fruit smoothie. He's constantly checking his phone.

Blanco texts him, "Be there in two minutes! What are you wearing?" he asks.

Antonio replies, "Black shirt, grey sweats."

An older Hispanic gentleman sporting a white polo shirt, blue jeans, and dad sneakers enters and Antonio looks up. He gives him thumbs up, but Antonio is still unsure if this is Blanco. The man raises his phone in the air and slowly points it in his direction kind of insinuating it's him. Antonio nods, and he walks to him with his right hand extended for a handshake. They greet one another.

"Juan, right?" Blanco confirms Antonio by his alias.

"Yeah, yeah, that's me."

They sit down and the waitress comes over smiling, kissing Blanco on the cheek. "Agua?" she asks in Spanish.

Antonio has been to this restaurant before, but he has never received a kiss from a waitress. She must know him personally, he thinks to himself.

"You want another smoothie, Juan?" he smiles.

"No, this is great. Thank you."

The waitress brings over Blanco's water and walks away immediately.

"So, Juan, let's get to it, yes?"

"Yes, please, that's why I'm here, but before anything, I speak Spanish…if you feel more comfortable," he reminds him.

"Oh, nice. Yes, either way. Are you Dominican?"

"Well, half Dominican, Colombian, and a sprinkle of Puerto Rican, too," Antonio jokes with the hand gesture.

"Good for you. I'm Colombian, but been here for the last 10 years. Make better money here, if you get what I'm saying. Speaking of money, I'm assuming that is why you are here, no?"

"Yes, Calbo told me you need a driver and like a security detail, someone to have around you?"

"Ahh, yes. Something like that, but for now I'll have you meet with Calbo's brother. The purpose of this meeting was to see if you are fit for what we need. Today you'll meet with Brandon, and you'll pick him up and drop him off and I'll have him pay you after that job's done."

"Today? Oh, um, ok?" he ponders.

"It's quick and it's early. You can go now, I'll text you the address and his number. You leave now you'll be done by 2pm the latest," he assures.

"Ok, cool," Antonio agrees.

"Let me be a little clear, Juan. You know you're here because I know you're an officer, that's why I asked for you. Just know I take this very serious. I'm about my money. Don't mess this up and you can also make a lot of money with us," he says.

"You can count on me," Antonio cheers.

"Good, keep in touch. Call Brandon and he'll give you instructions."

He gets up and shakes Antonio's hand, walks over to the register, and points to the table on his way out. Antonio sees the text from Blanco giving him Calbo's brother's number and address. When he goes to pay for his fruit smoothie the waitress says it's been taken care of by Blanco. Antonio walks out and heads to his car. It starts to rain. The second he closes the door his phone vibrates and it's a random number.

"Hello, who is this?" Antonio answers the phone.

"What's good, bro? It's Brandon. I'm on 207 street and Broadway. Call this number when you're downstairs, and try to get here quick cause I have to pick up my kids soon. We'll be in and out," the raspy voice demands on the other line.

"Oh ok, ok. Yeah, I can be there in less than 30. I'll hop on the Triborough Bridge then the Harlem River Drive."

"Copy, copy," Brandon agrees.

35 minutes pass and Brandon is outside on the phone with his brother Calbo, patiently waiting for Antonio to arrive. He sees someone at the corner and gets an incoming call from him, the timing couldn't be any better. He merges the call.

"That's you, right? Black Charger?" Brandon asks over the phone.

"Yeah, man. You're outside, right? Grey sweat suit?"

"Yeah, yeah. Yo, say what's up, Calbo on the other line right now. You called while I was on the phone."

"What's up, man! Listen, you be good. I got to get off the phone, but my little brother's going to take care of you, trust me," Calbo tries to comfort him.

"Yeah, copy. Later."

Antonio is eager to get off the phone since he knows jail phone calls are recorded. Brandon hops in the passenger seat and greets Antonio with a handshake. Brandon looks like the typical uptown young go-getter, sweat suit, big earrings, crispy haircut, and the latest sneakers. He resembles his older brother, the only difference is his head full of hair.

“What’s going on, my brother? Nice car, man. I know COs make money, but this is clean,” Brandon smiles checking out his ride.

“Yeah, man. I appreciate it. Talk to me, what are we doing because I’m kind of in a rush, too,” he tells him nervously.

“Let me run upstairs and get my bag. We drive to 125th and Broadway I give that to my aunt and we head right back and that’s it.”

Antonio nods as Brandon gets out and slams the door. Antonio suspiciously looks around his surroundings. He knows this block in particular is drug infested and notorious for drug activity. He used to play in basketball tournaments nearby back in high school. The 4 minutes Brandon takes seem like eternity. He gets back in, obnoxiously turns on the AC without asking, while holding a red book bag. Reclining his seat, he gives Antonio a nod.

“You ready, man?” Brandon questions.

“What’s the address?”

“Take the West Side Highway, I’ll tell you where to get off. I thought you were from Harlem,” he jokes.

They drive off and get unto the highway in an awkward silence. Brandon’s phone rings once again.

"Yeah, I'm 5 minutes away," he tells the person on the other line.

Antonio starts to sweat. He has a million thoughts running through his mind. Deep down, he's dying for this to be over. He cares less and less about the money at this point. Brandon signals him to get off the exit and they park along the water front. He gets out and takes the book bag with him, remaining on the phone.

"I'll be back in 5 minutes, bro. In and out," Brandon states.

He slams the door while Antonio's eyes are glued to the mirrors as he watches Brandon go into another car parallel to his. He notices it's a female in the driver seat and a male in the passenger. They pop the trunk and he throws the backpack in, greets them both, has small talk, and walks back towards Antonio.

"Yo, come meet my aunt, just in case you got to link and she might need you. Matter of fact, I'm going to have her come," he tells Antonio giving him no chance to chime in.

He waves for her to get out and walk towards them, and she does. A busty Hispanic woman with big brown eyes, black hair, and lots of make-up, wearing a sports bra and jean shorts.

She smiles, "Hey, how you doing? Lisa," she extends her hand and greets Antonio.

"What's up? Juan."

"You guys should exchange numbers. You know I be out of town, and this way if she needs you, you two can speak," he reminds.

"Okay cool, yeah," Antonio puts up the front that he's cool, calm, and collected.

They all leave and Antonio drives back towards uptown to drop off Brandon. He gets back a lot faster than the drive there, maybe in part because there's some weight lifted off Antonio's shoulders now since there's no book bag in the car. They arrive and Brandon hops out while taking yet another phone call. He tells Antonio to give him a minute while he lights a cigarette. Antonio remains still and anxious to leave the premises immediately. Brandon hangs up.

"Yo, man, see...1,2,3, told you. Listen, I'm going to set something up in a couple days. We might have to head downtown though, and then probably my aunt might link with you if anything."

He reaches into his pocket and pulls out two knots of money, throwing one of the knots on the passenger seat.

"I'll call you, man. Make sure you pick up," he tells him in a semi-dominant tone.

"Okay, yeah, no problem. See you later then," Antonio agrees and nods.

Brandon walks off into the building and Antonio speeds away as fast as possible. He gets on the highway and he still hasn't even counted the money. His adrenaline is pumping and his main objective is to head home to be far away from the scene. He parks up an exit away from his home, takes in a deep breath, and retrieves the money from the passenger seat. It's all $20 bills. He counts 125 $20 bills, $2,500 in 30 minutes. He can't believe it. His last check from the Department of Corrections was $1600 after his 80-hour week. This is crazy. He's flabbergasted, amazed, and in awe. This is his big break. With a side income like this, he can get his mother to move out of project housing, get the professional help his younger sister needs, and move himself out to save for a better future. He can't stop smiling. This was too easy, he didn't even touch anything, or even get out of his vehicle. This is easy money and he deserves this!

Just a 10 minute drive away, CO Jones sits in his vehicle outside Mya's building. He's anxious to have a one on one conversation about what she plans to do with her pregnancy. Mya knocks on the window and gets in.

"What's good? How you feeling? Jones asks.

"I'm fine. Just give me my money, I don't even want to be around you."

Jones reaches into his cargo pockets and hands Mya an envelope, "That's for the abortion and a little extra since I put you through all this nonsense," Jones tells her in a very low and timid tone.

She grabs it and walks out. Jones speeds off. Mya counts the cash slowly and it's $3,000. She smiles. Crossing the street, she sees Antonio exiting his car.

"Tony!"

He stuffs the cash he just counted in his pocket, startled from hearing his name yelled down the block.

"Hey, Mya! How you been?" he asks with a huge smile.

"Just hanging in there. How's Rikers treating you?" she questions.

"I love it. It gets hectic with all the violence and the gangs going at each other, but overall I make it work for me, you know?"

"Yeah, I feel you. You know a guy in your building named Flacko?"

He ponders for a second, "Yeah I do. Trinitario member, right?"

"Right, if you see him when you go back tell him call me ASAP!" she tells Antonio, not really fearing judgment.

"Call you? You guys are cool like that?" Antonio reverts.

"Yeah, kind of. He's my ex's friend. Tell him I said I can't be going up there like that anymore. I'm starting my GED courses, so he needs someone else."

Antonio's extremely confused, "Um ok, I got you. I'll tell him tomorrow."

She waves goodbye and they head their separate ways.

THE NEXT DAY

Antonio gets a call from Lisa, Calbo and Brandon's aunt. He answers and puts it on speaker while he gets dressed for work.

"Hey! Juan?" Lisa confirms.

"Yeah, what's good?" he answers her in a rush.

"Listen, I need you Tuesday and Friday either before or after work, whatever's best for you. Tuesday, just need you to take me to 42nd and 10th Ave and Friday I'll give you something, but won't go with you, just got to drop it off to Brandon. Every Tuesday and Friday, cool?" she asks.

"Yeah, um, okay. I just got to coordinate correctly."

"Sounds good, see you Tuesday!" she's excited.

FEW WEEKS LATER

Antonio's been running these transaction errands with Lisa and Brandon and has even met with other members of this organization, gaining payouts of $3,000 or better, and on a couple instances $7,300. He figures that the more they transport, the better the payouts get. He's been stacking this money up. On one of the very last transactions, he meets with Brandon again. They're parked up in the car together.

"Good looking, bro. I'll see you in a few days, but here, give this to Calbo. He needs it ASAP!"

Brandon hands him a small 3 inch by 2 inch box like package, wrapped in electrical tape.

"Yo, what is this?" Antonio grabs it.

"It's a little tobacco and weed, but trust me, it's compressed tightly. No smell, nothing," he assures him.

Antonio is very uneasy about this, "I mean, um, damn. I never brought anything in for anyone, and you know it's been a while since I've even seen Calbo. He's on the whole other side of the building."

"You a smart guy man, just figure it out. I gotta go," he brushes Antonio off.

Brandon walks out the vehicle and into his building, leaving Antonio with nothing except that mysterious package. He's stuck and unsure about how he's going to execute this. He was ok with just being a courier on the street, using his badge, gun, and car, but now he has to attempt to be a courier internally in Rikers. Something he's been approached to carry out numerous times and occasions in his early days fresh out of the academy. He's conflicted and drives off, putting the small package in his arm rest. First, he takes a quick smell of it. It's odorless and no bigger than a standard pack of cigarettes. He arrives to the parking lot of Rikers as he works the 1pm- 9:30pm shift. He hopes to bid for a position that has just opened up for mentally ill inmates serving Box time called RSU (Restrictive Housing Unit). The inmates with good behavior are allowed to come out of their cells and enter the dayroom for a few hours of the day. This helps depopulate solitary and slowly get them back to re-enter general population.

He walks toward the main entrance with the package in his back pocket, opposite from his wallet. He's unsure if the metal detector will sound; he becomes fidgety, but reminds himself to become calm.

The same old timer officer is at the front gate and greets everyone walking in, lawyers, civilians, two EMT workers who are here to transport an inmate from the clinic to the local hospital. Antonio grabs anything metal he might have on his person, keys, phone, and gum, and unfastens his belt to put them all through the machine. He clears the manometer with the package still in his back pocket. It doesn't ring, and he's relieved. He gathers everything and walks straight to his locker, maintaining calmness. He greets a few guys and goes straight to his post and bumps into Captain Davis.

"Sanchez, do me a favor. Go relieve the officer in dorm 10, the A-officer. She's about to be on a triple and needs to go home, and then I'll get a meal officer to take your place before the count," Captain Davis states.

"Yes, sir."

The way the stars aligned is crazy. Antonio was just sent to the same exact housing area Calbo is in, which means he can get rid of this package quick. He walks to dorm 10 and the female officer was already at the door waiting. She's been at work for 17 1/2 hours. She's dying to leave knowing she has to come right back in about 6 hours. She hands Antonio the keys and walks past him. Antonio walks inside and the inmates are getting ready for the institutional count, while the B-officer on the floor starts to close the dayroom and collects the receivers off the phone. He opens the A-station bubble.

Calbo walks up to the bubble all smiles, "What's good Sanchez? How you feeling?" Calbo asks.

"I'm good, man. Listen, can you clean the bubble for me? The last officer left all her garbage."

"Yeah, definitely! Let me grab the broom," Calbo is ecstatic.

He goes to the janitor's closet and grabs the cleaning supplies. Other inmates peek through and see what's going on, but they realize it's Sanchez, nothing out of the ordinary. Antonio walks into the staff bathroom located inside the A-station, grabs the package out his pocket, and throws it in the garbage can.

"Grab the garbage in the staff bathroom first and change the bag. It's there."

"Copy, copy," Calbo continues to cheese from ear to ear.

Calbo walks into the bathroom and retrieves the package, puts it in his basketball shorts, changes the bag, and goes back to cleaning. Mission complete. It's out of his hands now, so whether he gets caught with it or the search team finds it on Calbo's person, it has nothing to do with him.

"Yo, you feeling the other job?" Calbo quickly asks.

"Yeah, it's cool, can't complain," Antonio tells him nonchalantly.

"Listen, man, if you can't reach me, I need you to holla at Flacko. He's on the other side of the building. The shit on the outside is always ongoing, but whenever my peoples throw you something for me, reach out to Flacko or me. They told me you're friends with Mya, we all connected, bro. Let's build and get this money together. My court case looking good. I'll be out of here soon, trust me!"

"Oh, you know Mya?" Antonio questions.

"C'mon, bro. My name rings bells Uptown and in Washington Heights. I know everyone, I'm just on pause right now, feel me?" his cockiness seeps through his pores.

The B-officer comes into the bubble and Calbo walks out and puts the cleaning supplies back as if nothing's happened.

LATER THAT NIGHT

Mohammad walks into the deli, purchases water and some chips, asks for 6 pouches of loose tobacco, and pays. Walking home, his phone rings and it's Mya.

"Hey, sorry I'm having you go through all this. I been going through a lot and don't plan on going up to visit for a while, but you can pass by for the money tomorrow," she says.

"Yeah, that's fine. It's cool, just got to pack it correctly."

"Yeah, it's easy. Just unpack all of them and put them in a Ziploc and slowly pour a cup or two of water and compress it that way. It'll make it 10 times smaller and won't have a smell."

"Oh ok, ok. Yeah, I get it. Let him know I'll be working tomorrow so be ready for it," Mohammad tells her.

"He knows, I just got off the phone with em."

"Copy, see you tomorrow for the money."

Before hanging up, he gets an incoming call from Antonio. He switches calls.

"Yo, what's going on? Is that you walking down Broadway?" Antonio's voice projects over the speaker.

Mohammad looks around smiling, eating his chips and bag in hand, "Yeah! Oh, shit! You see me, where are you?" he smiles hard.

"I'm walking towards you. I just parked up,"

Antonio tells him.

He meets with Mohammad and they embrace each other with a brotherly hug.

"What you doing over here in my neck of the woods, bro ?" Antonio inquires.

"My grandmother lives down the block, you don't remember me telling you?" he points.

"Oh right, right. I just got out of work, heading home. You want to come upstairs?"

"I could for a few, got to run home and take care of some shit, you know," Mohammad states.

"What did you buy? A sandwich? Chips?" he interrogates.

Mohammad smiles, "I mean something like that. I'm going to keep it real with you, man, since you brought it up and basically know what's going on. I just grabbed some tobacco and yeah, you know what's next."

Antonio stares at him, but Mohammad is unsure how he's being perceived. Antonio looks around, "Come upstairs with me for like 10 minutes, just to talk in private real quick at least."

They cross the street and enter the building elevator, kids playing in the hallway and guys smoking weed in the lobby. They get to the apartment and Mohammed sits on the couch across from Antonio who grabs two beers.

"Yo, I really think you should chill out with bringing that shit in, bro. I'm going to try to get you in on what I'm doing, but you need to be serious about it."

"Bro! I'm down. I told you I really don't like doing this, but an extra $500-$700 a week helps, man."

"I agree and trust me, there's been endless times I've been asked, too, but the security shit I'm doing is less of a risk, in my opinion. I'm just a driver. I link with them, they drop off their shit, and I drive them back and that's it. Easy money."

He leans over to listen, "What's the numbers looking like?"

"I made $2,500 my first trip. It took no more than an hour to do," Antonio explains.

"What! Bro, I'm in!" he agrees right away.

"I'ma call them and see what's up with bringing you on."

In mid-conversation, as if they were being heard, the phone rings. It's Blanco. Antonio puts his finger up and tells Mohammad to be quiet.

"Hello?"

"What's going on, man? Quick question, I have a big run this week. You got anybody else with you in the same situation with the same credentials as you that can join after meeting with me first?" Blanco asks while his voice projects over the phone speaker.

"You read my mind, sir. I was literally going to bring this up to you the next time we spoke," Antonio tells him.

"You want to bring him and yourself tomorrow morning to meet. I just want to make sure he's reliable. You've proven yourself, but I'd like to meet him tomorrow, yeah?" Blanco asks.

Antonio is in disbelief, "Yes, perfect. Shoot me an address tomorrow and the time."

"Got it, see you later."

They hang up.

"Bro, this is crazy," Antonio says in shock.

"What the fuck happened, man?" Mohammad questions.

"The same shit I was just going to do, you know, get you in, the main guy called me to have me bring another guy in to expand and do drop offs more frequently. This is crazy, bro. You see, law of attraction is real, man!"

"I'm all in. When do we start? Tomorrow?" Mohammad's clearly excited.

"Yeah, man. Tomorrow, early I'm assuming. You're off work, right?" Antonio verifies.

"Yeah, I'm off."

They grab their beers and do a small cheer to their new endeavor.

THE NEXT DAY

Mohammad links with Antonio at the parking lot of a Home Depot that Blanco asked to be the meeting location. It's 10am. Blanco arrives in a brand new fully loaded jeep. Blanco texts Antonio to have them both enter his vehicle, and they do exactly that.

"What's going on, fellas? Juan, how are you?" Blanco smiles.

Mohammad looks at Antonio confused that he was referred to as Juan, but catches on quick.

"How you doing? Nice to meet you. I'm Mike."

"Mike, this is Blanco," Antonio formally introduces.

They all shake hands.

"Well, I want to make this quick. I have a lot of running around to do. Basically Mike, I been working with Juan here and he's caught on quick to things, pretty sure he broke everything down to you. I just needed to meet you in person. Also, if you don't mind, I'd like to take a pic of your ID with my phone. If you run away with my shit, I know where to pay you a visit, make sense?" Blanco sternly states the rules.

"Yeah, that makes sense I guess," Mohammad is concerned.

He removes his ID from his wallet and Blanco takes a pic of it, not really questioning it. His main focus is getting paid. Antonio agrees with a head nod that this is nothing, just go with the flow.

"You guys willing to do a quick run right now?" Blanco asks them both too see how loyal they truly are.

They do a quick glance at one another. Antonio's eyes widen.

"Um, yeah, I mean we are both off, I guess. It'll be quick right?"

"Quick, in and out test run, you know? I'm gonna throw the bag in your car, and you guys head out. It's literally a 15 min drive. I'll text you the address," Blanco assures.

They all exit the vehicle and both are extremely nervous. Blanco calls over Mohammad and has him psychically grab two bags from the trunk, something Antonio has never actually done. They throw it in Antonio's car and get the address through text.

"Hey, I'm doing something I rarely do, but I'm in a rush here. I'll pay you guys ahead, you pass this to the guy waiting. Here, take this."

Blanco hands them each an envelope. They hop in Antonio's car and drive off. They open the envelope on their way to their destination from the text. They have each been paid $3,000.

Mohammad is ecstatic, and it's all they talk about while driving to the drop off destination. They arrive and they see a heavy set black gentleman standing tall outside of his brand new G-wagon Mercedes Benz. They approach him and he signals it's him who they came to meet and drop off the goods to. They do exactly that. The man grabs the bag and shakes their hands; he throws the stuff in his car. They leave and hop back in their vehicle. Mohammad can't believe it's that easy.

"Wow, man. That was it?" Mohammad is in shock.

"I told you, bro. Look, 3k, just like that. Fuck with me from now on and you could make this money, man!" Antonio assures him.

"Definitely, I just got to bring this last little situation I got with a dude in there. It's crazy because I think he said you know his girlfriend who I would meet to get paid."

"Oh shit, Mya?" Antonio questions.

"Yeah, something like that," he tries to recall.

"You know what's crazy? The guy who put me on to this and stays in dorm 10, a week ago told me that they're all connected. I guess they belong to the same gang."

"Calbo, right?"

Antonio is surprised. "Yeah, him, small world. Well, listen man, do what you got to do, but every time there's a run and you're needed I'ma holla at you."

He drops off Mohammad and they head their separate ways.

For a few months, Antonio continues meeting with Mohammad for every run after that, except for a couple of instances where Mohammad wasn't present because of working a double on Rikers. Mohammed and him still supply Flacko and randomly meet with Mya and Calbo's associates on the inside just to keep a good rapport. They are all in cahoots with each other, and at this point, Antonio is making an easy $6,000-$11,000 weekly. He starts not knowing what to do with all this revenue. He purchases a new car, moves out of his mother's house, puts a down payment on a two bedroom condo, gives his mother a bi-weekly allowance, pays for a private tutor for his sister, and even starts going on mini vacations. Miami becomes like a second home for Antonio. He loves the nightlife out there and becomes some sort of like a playboy figure. Club and lounge hopping in L.A. and Vegas as well, all while still juggling his 9a-5p as a NYC Correction Officer. He's living his best life and hopes this never ends.

During all this success, Antonio acquires a bad drinking habit. He's never really been the club / lounge strip club type up until recently, but with so much income coming his way, he starts to get ahead of himself. He's doing bottle service and taking friends and girlfriends out to eat at lavish restaurants. He's having shopping sprees, buying jewelry, and blowing thousands of dollars on strippers. His new lifestyle is starting to become uncontrollable. Former CO Tiffany who lost her job and took up stripping has developed a newfound friendship at her new work place where Antonio is an elite customer. She becomes his partner in crime when it comes to bringing strippers around and popping bottles. She's not really sure what he's up to, but she's enjoying every dollar he has to spend. They start to have a romantic and sexual relationship and his new way of moving starts to spiral little by little. His depression and anxiety heighten as he copes with juggling crime and integrity. Months of this continues with no end in sight.

Almost two weeks pass and Antonio hasn't heard from Blanco, Brandon, Mya, the aunt or anyone. He decides to reach out to them. Financially, he's stacked enough money where he'd be fine for a long time, but for it all to just cease, he's starting to question things. Even while on Rikers, he has yet to see Calbo or Flacko. Mohammad is on a drought as well with bringing things on the inside. The jail has once again been on lockdown due to the extreme spike in weapons and violence.

After several attempts and days passing by, Antonio gets no call from anyone regarding what the next move might be. Finally, after everyone's phones being off for a period of days, he gets a call from a blocked number. He answers and it's Blanco's voice.

"Listen, sorry for the delay. I just had some bad business mess up my flow. Long story short, I'm not messing with the Dominican guys, you know. You get what I am saying?"

"Yeah, I understand. So, what now, it's over?" Antonio asks with uncertainty.

"It's never over. This Monday, after Father's Day, meet me at the Target parking lot on 225th and Broadway. All the way on the last level. This is big, I need you to be on time and your friend Mike, too. I can't have any mistakes with this trip. 8:30am, sharp," Blanco asserts,

"Yeah, man, definitely. See you tomorrow!"

Antonio hits up Mohammad with the news. They're both happy to know that they're getting some cash tomorrow. They've become so accustomed to their new way of living, and this was needed.

The very next morning, Antonio and Mohammed arrive there at 8:15am. Mohammed goes out for a cigarette while Antonio waits for the call by scrolling through pictures taken of him at the strip club a couple nights ago.

He receives a text from Blanco, "Be there in less than 10 minutes."

"Yo! He's on his way, you heard?" Antonio tells Mohammad.

Mohammad can't stop smiling, "I'm ready, man. It's my girl's birthday tomorrow, I need this bad."

"Same here. I put in for six days off next week. I plan on going to Miami for Fourth of July weekend," Antonio brags.

"I hear that, man."

A white truck arrives and parks five spaces away from them. Blanco rolls down his window.

"Before you grab everything, come and sit in the car. Let's talk before we head out," he shouts from his car window.

They both glance at each other and get in the car.

"I like this truck, man. I just got one. Pretty good on gas, right?" Antonio tells him.

"Yeah, I enjoy it myself. You might be able to grab another one after these next few ones. I've been dealing with some Mexicans and those guys are moving, but listen, you guys are going to Yonkers. Mike, you grab the blue bag. Juan, I need you to grab the brown one. Go there right behind you and open them up, so you guys see what you're working with," Blanco advises.

They do exactly that. They open the duffle bags and Antonio finds two compressed packs of white powder, a Ziploc filled to the brim of the same white substance, and another Ziploc full of white pills. Now he's anxious and he can sense that Mohammad feels the same way. Blanco tells them to type the address down on their phone.

"686 School Street. That's Yonkers. I'll drive behind you guys on this one. I'll explain why later. Also, I won't be paying you guys in cash right now, but you'll receive payment tomorrow, deal?" Blanco details.

"Yeah, definitely. We're not stressing over the pay; we know what's going on."

Blanco looks back, "Good, let's get to it then."

They all step out of the vehicle. The parking lot's empty as can be with the exception of a few scattered cars. Antonio looks around and secures his duffle. He looks at Blanco and looks at Mohammad.

"See you guys there?" Antonio questions.

"Let me run to the bathroom before heading out, you guys head there in your cars. Give me two minutes," Blanco glances around oddly.

They all nod. Mohammad walks side by side with Antonio to their car.

"Yo, what time you got? I left my phone in the car."

Antonio presses his Nike Fuel band to check. "It's 8:34," he says in a low tone.

In the split-second Antonio took to check his watch, a white Enterprise van with no windows screeches about 60 feet in front of them and the doors bust wide open. Three men in riot gear and bulletproof vests are pointing AK-47s with beams attached to them and stop Antonio and Mohammad in their tracks. They both freeze up and can't believe what's going down.

The men scream, “GET ON THE GROUND!!” three times.

Mohammad looks at them, then at Antonio thinking “what the fuck is going on!?”

Antonio looks at the agents and mentally tells himself to wake up from this dream, this nightmare.

Two other unmarked cars get to the scene, one on each opposite side of the Enterprise rental van. This is all happening in slow motion from Antonio’s perception. For him, his life is practically flashing before his eyes. He can’t fathom what’s transpiring.

After the last “GET ON THE GROUND,” Antonio gets on one knee. The second he does, the duffle bag with the drugs drops and so does he. He feels the knee of another man firmly press all of its weight on him while his elbow gets pinned to his back. He watches Mohammad going through the same motions. The man behind him strips him of his personal protection firearm, a Glock 19. He removes it from the holster on Antonio’s waist, disassembles the clip, empties the bullets in the head chamber, and hands it over to his partner. Antonio looks up and reads that all the agents around them have one thing in common, their vests read DEA. He knows DEA stands for Drug Enforcement Agency.

While all of this is going on, Antonio catches a glimpse of Blanco in a physical altercation with three other DEA agents who are struggling to get him out the vehicle. He figures they weren't going to let him go. A million things are going through his mind. He's scared, nervous, uneasy, uncomfortable, and really just numb.

The agents grab Mohammad first and throw him in one of the unmarked cars, then cuff Antonio and do the same thing. From his view, Blanco is finally apprehended and placed in a vehicle. He gets in and is seated next to a white heavy-set man in the backseat sporting a DEA vest, too. A minute or two pass and a young Asian female DEA agent enters the driver's seat and they head down the parking lot ramp. Antonio is mentally and physically drained, looking out the window, and it's only been, at most, 10 minutes.

"Hey, what precinct are we going to?" Antonio still feels like he's dreaming.

"Precinct?" the DEA agent responds with a grin on his face.

The DEA agent pulls out his badge from under his vest to show Antonio, the obvious. This is a federal agency.

"We're going to headquarters," he tells him.

They drive along the West Side Highway and all Antonio wants is for this to be over. He maintains his composure, but deep down he wants to scream and cry. They exit on 10th avenue and enter a dark parking lot, and what seems to be a maze of ramps and reposed exotic cars. Finally, they park and both agents escort him to the elevator. He doesn't see anyone else he's been apprehended with in sight. The elevator button has been pressed to floor 18. The doors open and a huge emblem of the same DEA badge is plastered on the opening wall of that floor. It's just a constant reminder of exactly where he is. He is escorted down a long hallway and then is placed in a bull pen that resembles a jail cell, bars and bench and all. The cuffs are taken off and he is asked to step inside of the holding cell. Antonio remains in complete disbelief.

Inside the DEA headquarters, over eight federal agents walk in and out of the room, all eyeing their latest catch. After 30 minutes, Antonio looks up and sees Mohammad strolling in escorted by two other agents and a female in a business suit with Blanco coming in right behind her, also handcuffed and escorted by another officer. They both get placed in separate bull pens to the right of Antonio's. There's an awkward silence, and Mohammad interrupts that.

Mohammad shouts, “Officers, can I make a phone call and get my lawyer up here, please?”

“Relax, no need to shout. Give us a minute and we’ll get you situated. Just chill,” one of the DEA agents tells him.

“Yo, man, what the fuck is going on?” Mohammad asks in a low, secretive tone.

He gets closer to Antonio’s side of the wall separating them, “This has to be a dream, man. How the fuck and what the fuck is happening?”

“Don’t say anything. Wait for your lawyer, okay?”

Antonio instructs him.

“Listen, guys, no talking. You’ll get your phone calls, just be patient. There’s a lot going on right now,” the other DEA agent states.

They remain quiet. Mohammad can’t stop pacing in his cell. Antonio just lies on his back and closes his eyes trying to wrap his head around everything that is going on. The woman in the business suit with no badge or ID displayed walks up to the bars and asks for Antonio to be placed in one of the rooms for a non-interrogation questionnaire. A female agent unlocks Antonio’s cell while another unlocks Mohammad’s. They exit and enter separate rooms.

The young agent, slim and blonde, possibly in her 30s, sits down at the table and grabs her chair to position herself to face Antonio.

"Have a seat. Look, this is not an interrogation. All I'm asking you is basic information, name, address, maiden name, etc. You have the option of answering or having a lawyer present, but in all honesty the faster you give me this basic information, the faster you get out of here. You can opt out and wait for your counsel, but that may take a few hours. Entirely up to you, but my suggestion is we do this quick," she explains.

Antonio remains stale, but nods his head in agreement. In his mind, they have that basic information by just looking at his driver's license, but it's whatever.

In a completely separate room, Mohammad sits with another female agent. She's West Indian, short, and petite. She goes through the same protocol. Once they finish the basic information paperwork, she gets up and two stocky football player built agents, both African American, stroll in and grab chairs to sit directly across from Mohammad.

“What the fuck, man? How did you get wrapped up in all this shit? You know the guys you were with?” questions DEA agent #1.

Mohammad stays quiet, maintaining composure.

“We obviously know you and your boy are partners. You guys work on Rikers, right? I’m assuming you guys were just paid security?” interrogates DEA agent #2.

He holds his silence; he knows it’s better to just wait for his lawyer. They continue to ask questions and assume the answers, to get him to break.

“Can I please get on the phone and call a lawyer?” Mohammad asks.

“Definitely, but again, do you even know who you two were around? This guy you guys were working under, we’ve had surveillance on him for over a year. He’s big time. We were just waiting for a perfect time and didn't expect you two there. You don't want to clear your name of this CO Mohammad?” the DEA agent #2 presents to Mohammad.

Mohammad shakes his head, “Listen, sir, I’ll gladly have this conversation with you once I have proper representation. I know the law.”

“The law!? If you knew the law, you wouldn't be using your power as a member of service to transport cocaine for a Colombian drug lord in New York City!" DEA agent #1 sternly shouts.

They stare each other down as agent#1 is held back by agent #2.

In Antonio's room, two other DEA agents enter, one Hispanic male in his 40s covered in tattoos and one white male, bald-headed and in his 50s.

"How old are you, man?" the Hispanic DEA agent asks.

"Sir, I been asking for a lawyer since I've arrived here," Antonio reminds him.

"That's already been requested. I'm pretty sure they spoke to those correction union guys to come get you out of here quickly," the Hispanic agent tells him.

"You know you just got caught up in us infiltrating that older gentleman you were with, right? He's no fucking joke. We know you probably have no idea. Regardless, save us and yourself the energy by telling us how you guys met because you see that lady out there in the suit?" the white agent starts to inform Antonio.

Antonio stares blankly at the wall as both agents pace around him.

“She’s the Assistant District Attorney for Special Narcotics of New York City. She’s just as confused as us. We didn't set that whole ordeal up for you or your partner. This was to grab that guy who we’ve been eyeing for a while now. She’s willing to let you both walk away as if this didn't even occur, but you both have to give us the detailed information we’re asking of you,” the agent continues.

“Listen, man. You're a correction officer for the city, you make decent money, you're what? 24-25?”

“Just tell us what happened and how all this even came about? Did you know there were two kilos of pure cocaine in that duffle bag? I don’t believe you really did, and the DA doesn't think so either, so just run down how this whole shit transpired,” the Hispanic agent proceeds in getting information out of Antonio.

“Well, before anything,” Antonio starts.

Both agents are open ears.

He sighs, “I need my lawyer, plain and simple.”

The Hispanic agent storms out the room, the White agent shakes his head and laughs briefly as he also steps out the room.

“You’re making this hole deeper, Sanchez. We tried being nice; but apparently, you don’t know what you have truly gotten yourself into.”

“I bet, call me a lawyer,” Antonio defensively tells them.

The white agent closes the door and about 3 minutes pass before he walks back in alone.

“Oh, and guess what? Your partner, your friend, your boy, or whatever he is, he’s in the next room singing like a bird at an American Idol audition. You’re fucked big time, Mr. CO!” he taunts.

Antonio puts his head down and rests it on the table. He’s scared to death, more so because he knows this bad dream is an actual reality and it is only the very beginning. The Hispanic agent walks back into the room and cuffs him to take him into another room for finger printing and processing. They take his mug shot, and use the computerized finger print computer. Another high-tech machine scans both his eyes and uses a facial recognition scan for their federal data base. He doesn't see Mohammad or Blanco anywhere. The female Assistant District Attorney, a very young white brunette with hazel eyes, walks in and watches the whole process.

"Mr. Sanchez, you do know you're facing 15 years for your involvement in trafficking narcotics, right? My agents are allowing you to offer some insight only because you are, well, you were, I don't know about after this, a New York City Correction Officer. The Department of Investigation is also here if you'd like to speak with them and make this ordeal better than it currently is. I'm granting you one last opportunity," she tells him in the sternest and most serious voice she has.

"I respectfully decline, ma'am. All I'm asking for is to speak to a lawyer, use the phone, and use the restroom. Thank you."

She walks out and slams the door.

"You got the wrong one mad my friend. I've never heard her give anyone some slack and offer them a chance. You must like losing, huh" the Hispanic agent reminds him sarcastically.

He cuffs Antonio again and escorts him back to the holding pen to use the toilet there, out in the open with no privacy at all. Antonio's anxiety rises. The Hispanic DEA agent stands at the bars on the opposite side watching him urinate.

"Hey man? That car you had, that shit is clean, bro. It barely had 200 miles on it. Did you just purchase? Cause if you did, it belongs to us now. Also, they fucked those seats up. The dog tore up everything looking for more drugs, but I guess you want to wait for that lawyer, huh" he continues to taunt.

He flushes the toilet.

About 2 hours go by, still no sight of the other two guys, just federal agents walking around, in and out of rooms and the Assistant District Attorney eye balling him from time to time. She gives the signal to get him out of here and two NYPD officers in plain clothes walk in as the female DEA agent unlocks the bull pen telling Antonio to step out. He does so and the NYPD officer handcuffs him and escorts him out of the room, back into the hallway where they head towards the elevator and exit into an unmarked car. They drive back onto the highway for two exits and arrive at the Tombs (Manhattan Detention Complex). Antonio was here many years ago one night in his teens when he was arrested for not having identification on him while playing basketball in the park with his friends. That case was thrown out and he remained in central bookings for only a weekend.

His side of the car door gets opened and they all enter through a side door bypassing other NYPD officers and guys who have just themselves been arrested and are

being detained. They place him in a whole separate cell pen by himself, being watched by none other than a Department of Corrections officer who has yet to learn who Antonio is. He takes advantage of the payphone in the cell and calls the only person he knows will have his back, his mother.
He dials and waits, slowly his eyes water with embarrassment.

"Hello?" Ana answers.

"Mami? It's me, Tony," he speaks with a crack in his voice.

"Tony? Where are you? Whose number is this? Are you ok?"

"Mami, listen, I'm in trouble. I have no idea what's going on. I went to do something with this guy for a few bucks and the cops came. It was a trap and they arrested me, but I have no idea what this is about. They have me in the courts downstairs and I don't know what they're going to charge me with. They found drugs; I think. It's bad, mami. If you can come downtown and get a lawyer, please. I should be getting arraigned soon and they'll give me a bail to leave," he tells her evidently destroyed by it all.

"Tony! Are you fucking kidding me? What guy? Why are there drugs? I'm so confused," she yells.

“Mami, please just come to the Tombs before I see the judge. Call the bail bonds guy. There’s money in my sneaker box, cash and some jewelry. Bring everything with you. Call my friend Tiffany, she can go with you. Please, just come.”

“Oh my god, Tony! What did you do, please Jesus Christ, please why?” she grieves.

“I’m going to call Tiffany to meet you at the house, mami. I will call you back in a few minutes. I love you. I’m so sorry, mami, please. I’m sorry, forgive me. All I wanted to do was give you and Marisol a better living. Just hurry and get everything together and come, please. I’ll explain in person after I get out. I don't want to speak too much over the phone. I love you!”
he hangs up and tears rolls down his eyes. His head is against the wall.

He’s interrupted by one of the COs passing by, “Yo! You’re Sanchez?” asks the random correction officer.

“Yeah, that’s my last name.”

“You’re an officer?” he continues.

“Yeah, I'm a CO,” Antonio looks around after saying it.

"Bro, you're on the news. They're saying you got caught with drugs, like keys of coke on your way to the Island, bro," he tells Antonio.

"Nah, it's a crazy misunderstanding. It's not even like that."

"Channel 4,5, and 7 saying it's four of you that got arrested. Man, I'm not judging. Let me call the union representatives for you. This is bugged out. You want something to eat or drink, I got you," he tells him.

"Please, man, it's been a hectic day."

That same second, Mohammad hits the corner and is placed in the same cell. They both look at each other, sharing the same emptiness and desperation. He goes straight to the phone and calls his mom to explain to her exactly what happened.

Antonio just listens to Mohammad trying to calm his mom down over the phone. She is screaming in anger, questioning how dumb he must be. He finally hangs up on her and the CO comes and brings them both deli sandwiches and sodas. He's accompanied by the Union President and a union representative and two lawyers. The bull pen is opened and they all sit on the bench in an attempt to prepare for what's next. A bald Caucasian male in crispy navy-blue Brooks Brothers suit extends his hand out to Antonio and introduces himself. His expensive Rolex peeking through his shirt cuff.

"Sanchez, correct? I'm Attorney Richard Peters. I will be representing you as council for arraignment purposes tonight and it is entirely up to you if you'd like me to represent you thereafter," Attorney Peters says.

Simmons interjects, "Sanchez, listen to me. This man is not your regular attorney. He's a heavy hitter. I've used him in the past and he's gotten me out of deep shit. For your next few court dates, the union will compensate. Tell him briefly what transpired and any key points he should know. We're going to get you a bail and see what the judge says moving forward. I gotta run. The mayor has a meeting tonight and I will get more information on your situation through him, ok?"

"Yes, sir," he nods nervously.

The attorney huddles closer to Antonio while the union rep and President Simmons speak briefly to Mohammad, reiterating the same exact thing.

The court room is packed with press, civilians, and lawyers. The judge is arraigning people back to back. Both Mohammad and Antonio are handcuffed and waiting for the court officer to escort them to stand in front of the judge. Antonio tries to get a peek to see if his mother is there; praying she did exactly what he asked of her and got a hold of the bail bonds man.

The court officer signals for them to step up both at the same exact time. Antonio sees his mom and can tell she's been crying hysterically. Tiffany stands to the left of her, wiping her tears after watching him stroll in cuffed. He's positioned to give them his back and stands directly in front of the judge. The lawyer steps up and whispers in both their ears.

"Listen, guys. Legally, I can only represent you both for arraignment only. I will be assigned to only one of you for the next court date, the other will get a lawyer by the union or you can hire your private one after today. This judge is a real bitch, excuse my French. I've been around her, she's stern. The Assistant District Attorney will ask her to deny bail and read the count or counts they plan on charging you with. Once that's said, the judge will set a bail. It's your first time being arrested so by law she needs to offer a bail. Let's wait," Attorney Peters explains.

The judge takes a small water break and reviews the papers placed in front of her. The Assistant District Attorney who Antonio met at the DEA headquarters walks in to the right of them with papers and files in hand. The court becomes noisy with people snickering and having small talk conversations. The press is camera ready and a few photographers from the local press take random pictures.

"Order in my court. ADA, are you ready to present?" shouts the white female judge.

"Yes, your Honor, ADA Lisette Burks representing the office of Special Narcotics Manhattan North District, presenting the City of New York vs. Antonio Sanchez and the City of New York vs. Rakim Mohammad. Both are charged with A1 Criminal Possession of a Control Substance and A1 Criminal Sale of a Control Substance as defined in NYS criminal law 220.21, 220.43. The office of Special Narcotics requests no bail, your Honor, due to both defendants being members of service and currently being employed by the New York City Department of Corrections. Both defendants can be proven to have abused their power to commit said acts and both currently possess active passports and are deemed flight risks. Defendant Sanchez in the last 120 days has taken flight to major cities such as Miami, Vegas, and Los Angeles with accumulated finances from his participation as a courier for a major drug trafficker known to the Special Narcotics office," the Assistant District Attorney opens up mercilessly.

The judge opens her eyes and takes off her glasses glancing quickly at both Antonio and Mohammad.

"Your Honor, Attorney Peters ESQ of Marksman & Sons Law Firm representing dual defendants for arraignment purposes only. Both have allowed me to represent them under consent for this hearing, and jointly and separately enter a plea of not guilty, your Honor." Attorney Peters said.

"I will allow counsel to represent both defendants for arraignment purposes only. ADA suggests no bail be set. Before my decision, would counsel briefly express why that might be unjust?" asks the judge.

"Yes, your Honor, thank you. Both defendants are college educated, hardworking members of service who have never been convicted of any crimes in their past. They do not pose as a flight risk, despite their travels, and have both served their community along with not being a dangerous threat to society in that they both do not possess any violent past behaviors. I ask you to oversee a bail to both to continue court proceedings at your earliest convenience from the luxury of their respected homes," states Peters.

The judge puts back on her glasses and looks at the paperwork given to her by the ADA.

“I’ve come to a decision to set a bail for both defendants based on the severity of the charges pending to $750,000 bond, $500,000 cash. If defendants cannot proceed with said amount, they will be placed in involuntary protective custody due to their occupations at the moment for their respective safety. Dismissed,” the judge announces.

The ADA holds back her grin while Antonio, Mohammad, and their lawyer walk off in shock down the aisle. Ana does nothing but shake her head and cry as Tiffany attempts to console her. She waves to Antonio as he’s escorted away.

Back at the holding pen, this one with no payphone, a million things are running through their minds. Antonio needs to get ahold of his mother to get this bail package, he’s thinking of what exactly he might need. The lawyer comes after a few minutes.

“Listen, guys, that’s an extremely high bail for the type of crime you’re being charged with. This is a scare tactic. We’re scheduled to go back to court next Tuesday. I will speak to your mothers and see what we can do in hopes of asking the judge assigned to you for a bail request. This last judge was just an arraignment judge so next week I’ll have more clarity. I have both your families’ information.

Mohammad, I won't be your attorney, but one will be assigned to you and we both will come visit you tomorrow, latest Wednesday," Peters explains to them.

"Court next week? Wait, so we're in jail till next week?" Mohammad questions with anxiety.

"Unfortunately, unless either of you can make this $750,000 bond. Remember this is a drug case so the courts are going to ask for validity, meaning they want bank statements, tax returns, proof of income for every dollar. Most bail bonds will charge 10% non-refundable, meaning you'd put up $75,000 to never get back. Just be patient and let's get to the next court date for a bail reduction hearing to see what your judge has to say then because this is truly excessive," Peters breaks it down to them.

Antonio shakes his head, "This is fucking crazy, man. You think we're staying here in the Tombs?"

"From what I've usually seen when past correction staff get into a situation, they get sent to either Nassau County in Long Island or Westchester County Jail due to the conflict of interest. Since you guys are guilty till proven innocent, you're both technically still on the job just probably facing suspension. Sanchez, you're cool with Simmons. He'll reach out to you and give you more details regarding that," Peters informs them.

“Just please keep in contact with my mom, man, please. Also, the girl she was with, fill her in if she doesn't understand fully. Tiff can reiterate slowly,” Antonio explains.

“Not an issue. See you tomorrow. Regardless of where you may land, for sure those are your options. Stay strong, we’ll work on this bail and we’ll gather more information. See you soon,” Peters tells them.

Peters walks out and the tension is giving them both a pounding headache. After waiting for over 10 hours, they both fall in and out of sleep in the holding pen. Two officers walk in with hand and leg cuffs in hand.

“Sanchez, Mohammad!” asks the transportations officer. “You got to use the bathroom, use it now. We’ll be taking you guys.”

Antonio yawns, “You know what facility we’ll be going to?”

“We’re not technically supposed to be telling anyone for security purposes, but you guys are still one of us, regardless. Westchester County, and honestly not a bad spot. It’s cleaner and more organized than here or the Island, trust me. I take guys there all the time. They even brag about the food being amazing, so let’s get going. It’s about 40 minutes away," says the other transportation officer.

They open the cell and slowly place the hand and foot cuffs on them, all parties become slightly uncomfortable.

In the eyes of the transport officers, they are still part of the team despite what the news channels might report. Who are they to judge? On Antonio and Mohammad's end, it's more embarrassment than anything. They're placed in the NYC Department of Corrections van. The vessel they would normally drive, transporting inmates to court or the hospital has now become the van transporting them who are currently viewed as inmates themselves. It's unsettling.

They arrive to Westchester County Jail and it's approximately 3am. At this point, they just want a pillow to rest on until the morning comes and they see their attorney. They go through the process of being asked a few questions by the Sergeant at this facility who already knows they are employed correction officers currently in custody. Sergeant Campbell is a Jamaican-American stocky male with tamed dreads and a neatly kept beard. Stern, but fair, aura, he interviews them both. He seems compassionate and sincere about the whole ordeal.

"What size suits would you say you both are? Large? XL?" Sergeant Campbell asks.

"I'll take an XL," Antonio says.

"Large please" Mohammad tells him simultaneously.

He calls on one of the county working inmates to retrieve those sizes.

"Last few questions, you can opt to speak and answer privately or jointly here in this room. Do either of you fear for your safety? If so, you would be placed in Protective Custody. I personally suggest you both go at least till your next court date, so honestly I'm asking because I am required by law to do so. Regardless of your answers, the Warden of this jail is placing you in involuntary PC," Sergeant Campbell explains.

Antonio becomes concerned, "Is it a 24hr lock down?"

"No, it's far from. Just escorted movement, separate visiting and recreation, nothing major. You'd honestly be around other high-profile inmates like yourselves."

"So, basically, no choice to say no, correct?" Mohammad asks.

"Not until we all get clarity on what's going on, and you guys won't be here long. I assume until after you post bail, right? So, let's play it smart and do PC for a few days."

They receive their jumpsuits and are escorted to the PC housing area. The transport officer from the Tombs were right, this jail is a million times cleaner and more organized than Rikers. There's even cameras everywhere. They have a video conference computer in their dayrooms for video visits with their family. This is all just as shocking as the actual reality of them being in bright orange jumpsuits getting walked to their jail cell for the night or possibly next couple nights till next week's court.

They get placed in their cells outside of the housing area since they are in Involuntary Protect Custody. They won't be in the actual housing area until they become fully assessed. The rooms are huge and they both have two windows. It's almost equivalent to a small studio. The toilet and sink are also in there. Only thing missing is the shower, which is located in the room to their left. It's 4am so it's pitch black, but the CO in charge of that block shows them that their light switch is on the outside of the door that they can turn on / off as they please. The doors lock. They both realize they went from doing the count to actually being the ones on the count. They make their beds with the sheet and blanket set up they were given downstairs in the intake area.

"Yo, A!" Mohammad whispers.

"Yeah?"

"I'm going to say a prayer for us, man. I have faith we're going to be ok. We just have to go through the motions, but at least we're not alone."

"Yeah, I know. I'm going to do the same, let's just try to jump on the phone tomorrow. Our moms are hurting tonight, probably more than us."

"I know, man. Let's hope the lawyers come, too."

They lie in bed and stare at the ceiling, each in their own mind in their own cell, just trying to piece together how this whole ordeal transpired and most importantly what's next. Antonio turns off his light and looks out his window. He begins to cry like a baby. He keeps reminding himself how stupid, how selfish, how dumb he truly is to have thrown everything away.

Three hours later, it's daylight and the doors are knocked and open. CO Manucci, an average built bald-headed Italian-American male, stands by the door with an inmate serving breakfast with the tray of cereal, a cinnamon roll, two milks, and croissant in hand.

"Hey, you want breakfast or not, guy?" Manucci shouts.

Antonio gets up quick, "Yes, um yeah, what time is it?"

"7:15am. Listen, you just got it. Eat this quick. I'll get you both on the phone before I lock out the house. Sergeant Campbell told me you didn't get a chance last night. This is my steady housing area. I run a tight shift, I'm fair, everyone here is fairly respectful. You work with me, I work with you. I explained it to your partner already, he goes on the phone first and then you, got it?"

He locks the door again. Antonio devours the food. It's actually not that bad. He uses the bathroom and washes his face, in hopes to get out and use the phone and call his mom to give her a peace of mind that he's ok despite the situation. All he has in mind is bailing out.

Inside the dayroom, Mohammad hangs up the phone after speaking to his mom. Antonio walks in and looks around and makes his way to the phone as well. He dials.

"It's all over the fucking news, man. My mom is tripping, everyone's tripping. It was front page on The Post, The Daily News, Channel 4, 5, and 7. They keep titling us 'Corruption Officers' and 'Trafficking Officers.' The DA spoke about us in a press conference, it's everywhere!" he tells Antonio.

"Fuck, man. Are you fucking serious? I'm going to call my mom. I hope she has this phone shit set up, let me see."

He dials and it rings. He hears the automated operator, then it connects.

"Tony?!" Ana picks up worried.

"Hi, mom. Any word from the lawyer or any information?"

"Tony, this is not something minor. What did you get yourself into, papi? This is all over the news, every channel! Tiffany told me all over the internet! Listen, I'm coming tomorrow to see you and bring you underwear and shirts, okay?" she sounds defeated.

"Damn, man. I was hoping to see you today. What did the lawyer say after I got arraigned? Have you spoken to the bail bondsman?"

"He told me wait so we can get it lowered. It's almost a million dollars, Tony!"

"Okay, ma, ok. I'm sorry I'm putting you through this. I have faith it's going to be okay, but I'm sorry. Please forgive me."

"I will come by tomorrow, Tony. Early in the morning. Let's see if your friend can bring me, ok?"

CO Manucci walks into the dayroom, "Sanchez! You have an attorney visit. The escort officer is on his way up. Hang up the phone," Manucci shouts.

He gives the CO a nod, "Ma! My lawyer's here. Let's see what he says, ok? I'll call you in a few. Pick up, ok?"

Antonio is called by the escort officer and given his ID to clip on his chest. They enter the elevator and go down to the visitor area. There's a lot more movement in the corridors now that it's the morning time. He can sense the staff there knows exactly who he is. He enters the visitor area and all eyes are on him, inmates and staff alike. He sees Peter in a fresh charcoal suit, walking in with a manila envelope in hand. They both enter a private room with a glass door for client and counsel privacy from everyone else.

"How are you feeling?" Peter questions, already knowing the obvious answer.

"Confused, desperate. Fucked up is an understatement."

They shake hands and sit at the table across from one another. Peters places the folder on the desk and opens it.

"Here's what I came here to inform you about, the reason why your bail was set so high is for one, you are a flight risk due to the money they claim you've made in the past year, your occupation, and your past travels. For two, you were indicted by the grand jury for A1 Criminal Possession and A1 Criminal Sale, both the top and highest drug charges in New York, right under Major Drug Trafficker. This is no small time case Sanchez, you're all over the media. They've shown your face everywhere. The Department of Investigation and DEA representative spoke alongside the District Attorney of Manhattan and ADA of the Special Narcotics Task Force about you shortly after your arraignment," Peters states.

Antonio is in disbelief, "So, there's no chance of the bail reduction the next time we go to court?"

"Honestly, I don't even want to ask. They may revoke it indefinitely and we only get one chance, but I represent you. If we get there and you feel you want to ask, we can request it there. My opinion, it's not worth it. On another note, tell me how you got to know this other guy, not your partner, but the other guy. You didn't notice he wasn't arraigned with you? Want to know why?" Peters tells him and takes in a deep breath preparing for what he's about to say.

"Throughout my 18 years as an attorney and six of those years working alongside the DA's office and prosecuting people, I can assure you this was a sting operation. It's obvious, from the outside looking in, that guy you ran around with was in on the whole thing. I'm not 100% sure if he's a federal informant or an undercover, but he's definitely in on it. My question to you now is how did we get here? How did you and the other guy meet with him? Who introduced you? Give me a rundown of everything, the more I know the better my argument in getting you out of here and worst case, getting you the least amount of time offered if and when going to trial is a smart option."

"Okay, so..." Antonio allows all this information to sink in.

As Peter grabs his pen and notepad, Antonio explains everything in as much detail as he can possibly recall. The council visit lasts over 2 hours, full of constant questions and answers. Council visits, unlike regular friends and family visits, are not timed so Antonio takes full advantage of giving key details so his lawyer can put together the pieces to this complicated puzzle. Peters has literally used up almost his entire notepad at this point.

"Wow, ok. Well, listen, I will be in contact with mom, and I will see you Wednesday. You should tell your mom to bring you a button-up shirt and some slacks, if possible. It won't do much for the judge, but just in case the press is there and decide to take pictures. I will request for them not to be, but that is up to the judge. Hang in there buddy, see you soon!"

They depart and Antonio heads back and gets escorted upstairs. He gets to the housing area and doesn't see Mohammad. The door is open and he walks into the dayroom, the three phones are being utilized by other inmates who eye ball him as he grabs a chair and watches Sports Center with everyone else. He's cautious of his surroundings and makes sure he grabs a chair not belonging to anyone. Being a correction officer on Rikers has made him privy to jail etiquette, and he knows taking someone's chair can lead to beef. Mohammad strolls in and has already made friends with two guys at the table. He was in the shower and Antonio asks to go shower as well. The phone in CO Manucci's office rings mid-conversation.

Manucci picks up the phone, "Again? Ok, yeah, I'll tell him. He's dressed, tell the escort officer to come back."

He hangs up, “You’re going to have to shower after your next visit, Sanchez. You got called back down.”

He’s confused, “Visit? My lawyer again?” Antonio asks.

“They didn’t say. The escort officer should be right back up so just wait at the gate.”

He does exactly that. The officer opens the gate and they go through the same motions and walk through the corridor back to the visitor floor. He’s asked to sit at a table with two empty seats. After 5 mins, he sees his visitors. It’s his mom and his friend Tiffany. He holds back his tears as he doesn't want to show emotion around the other inmates. The CO guides them to the table. They all embrace with hugs and kisses, both of them crying and sobbing.

Crying nonstop, “Hi, Papi!” Ana shouts.

“How you feeling?” Tiffany leans in for a hug.

They all sit.

“Just a lot going on at once, it’s overwhelming, and I just don’t know what’s next, you know?”

“I brought you underwear, papi, and court clothes, okay. They didn't let me bring the sneakers because I didn't have no receipt, but I’ll do so this weekend, ok? I called about your car and they said I can pick it up this Friday at 8am. They said I was lucky because if you owned it they wouldn't give it back, but since you leased it, it belongs to the bank. Tiffany was able to bring me today. I thought I had to wait till tomorrow to see you because the visits are by last name. I'm allowed to come any day if you been here for less than 72hrs, no matter what day," Ana tells her son.

"Wow, really? Thank you, ma. How'd you know I needed court clothes and the car stuff? How'd you get all the info?"

"Tony, unfortunately, I know how this goes from your father years ago and your brother. I didn't expect to be here for you, but I am your mother. I'll never want you to be uncomfortable and I will never hold anything against you. I will judge your actions but never your character, ok?" Ana whispers.

"Thank you, mami, thank you," he becomes emotional.

"You've got a lot of support, Tony, don't ever forget that," Tiffany reminds him.

They continue the visit for the next 45 minutes. This time they only have an hour. Antonio explains what happened during the visit with his lawyer, and he briefly discusses with them how he even got to this point. They share a quick prayer and the visit is over. They hug and kiss and depart. Antonio goes through a strip search, something he detested doing as an officer himself. A grown man forcing another grown man to take off his clothes due to the probability that he might be in possession of contraband, doesn't sit well.

He is given all the property his mom and Tiffany had dropped off, and he heads back upstairs and jumps in the shower. After a busy morning of seeing his lawyer and loved ones, he feels a little weight off his shoulders, but not entirely. He showers and ask to lock back in. He's not interested in watching TV and has no use for the phone for the day. He just wants Wednesday to come quickly, for clarity. He eats lunch, which is a chicken patty and some bread, and takes a nap.

Five days pass with them in county jail. Their court date is tomorrow morning. The PC housing area they've been housed in is pretty quiet for the most part. An argument here and there over dominos, poker, or the phone, but other than that, there haven't been any physical altercations. A few alarms throughout the rest of the building, but they're just used to it. The COs at Westchester County have been overly respectful and understanding. Antonio and Mohammad are both grateful and thankful, but even still, want out.

Downstairs in the intake area, Mohammad and Antonio change from their bright orange jumpsuits into the court clothes their mothers have brought them. They see the NYC Correction Officers arrive and get shackled to make their way downtown. There's traffic so it's about an hour drive. The car ride is fairly quiet. They do nothing but stare at freedom outside the window; kids attending their last week of school, people rushing to their office jobs, everyone's on the move. They haven't seen the city in over 6 days, but it feels like months.

They arrive. They head upstairs to the 11th floor and are placed into a bullpen, a few NYC COs walk by and shake their heads in disappointment. Captain Mitchell, who had transferred here a few weeks ago, comes to check in on them. She obviously heard the news and the COs in the staff room next to her office are pretty loud gossiping about the arrival.

"Sanchez," Mitchell gets his attention. She walks to the gate.

He looks up, "Hi, Capt."

"How you holding up? Where do they have you guys? Westchester?" she asks, making small talk.

"Yes, ma'am."

"Listen, we all have a fuck up moment. Don't let this bring down your spirit. I spoke to your cousin, she's telling you to do the same. You guys want something to eat? I'll bring you a bagel and coffee or juice, ok?"

"Thank you, Capt.," Antonio is extremely appreciative.

Two hours pass and they had breakfast, outside food which was much needed. They both lie on the hard-concrete benches and wait to get called in. Attorney Peters walks in and so does another attorney for Mohammad.

"Good morning, guys. Listen, we should be up in 10-15 minutes. You both got lucky with Judge Michaels. He's a very understanding judge. There might be press, but I'll request removal. Remember, it's entirely up to him. Let's hear what the ADA has to say and from there we'll make a decision on a bail reduction application, cool?" Peters explains.

The second that the lawyers exit, a court officer comes and calls them in. Antonio mentally asks God to help him and have his back. It seems like Mohammad does the same. They get hand cuffed and are both escorted to see their moms. Antonio sees two of his childhood friends and Tiffany there for support. Judge Michaels is a white-haired man in his 60s sporting glasses and a yellow polo shirt, not the black cape you usually expect a judge to wear. The ADA is also there with two other gentlemen in suits. The Stenographer is there ready to type and the judge secretary is handed a few documents by the ADA.

"Good morning, Supreme Court of the State of New York, County of New York Special Narcotics Parts, The People of the State of New York against Antonio Sanchez, Rakim Mohammad, Mya Suarez, Danny Rios, as defendants. Indictment No.2957/2014," shouts the court secretary.

Antonio eyes widen with astonishment.

"Honorable Michaels Presiding," Michaels awaits ADA Burks to present her claim.

"Good morning, Honorable Michaels. Lisa Burks for the DA's office of Special Narcotics, New York's Northern District, hereby voluntarily disclose a superseding indictment against all 4 co-defendants presented to you today on June 29th, 2014. All counts have been presented in front of a grand jury your Honor," says the ADA.

The court officer grabs a folder and hands it to the secretary to read. She stands up and nods at the stenographer to see if she is ready.

"CONSPIRACY IN THE SECOND DEGREE (2 COUNTS SANCHEZ AND MOHAMMAD, 1 COUNT

SUAREZ & RAMOS), CONSPIRACY IN THE FOURTH DEGREE (ALL DEFENDANTS), CONSPIRACY IN THE FIFTH (ALL DEFENDANTS), CRIMINAL POSSESSION OF A CONTROLLED SUBSTANCE IN THE FIRST DEGREE (1 COUNT SANCHEZ AND MOHAMMAD), CRIMINAL POSSESSION OF A CONTROLLED SUBSTANCE IN THE THIRD DEGREE (1 COUNT SANCHEZ & MOHAMMAD), ATTEMPTED CRIMINAL POSSESSION OF A CONTROLLED SUBSTANCE IN THE FIRST DEGREE (1 COUNT SANCHEZ & MOHAMMAD), ATTEMPTED CRIMINAL SALE OF A CONTROLLED SUBSTANCE IN THE FIRST DEGREE (1 COUNT SANCHEZ), ATTEMPTED SALE OF A CONTROLLED SUBSTANCE IN THE SECOND DEGREE (2 COUNTS SANCHEZ, 1 COUNT MOHAMMAD, SUAREZ, RIOS), ATTEMPTED CRIMINAL POSSESSION OF A CONTROLLED SUBSTANCE IN THE THIRD DEGREE (4 COUNTS SANCHEZ, 2 COUNTS MOHAMMAD, SUAREZ, RIOS), BRIBE RECEIVING IN THE THIRD DEGREE (4 COUNTS SANCHEZ, 3 COUNTS MOAHAMMAD), BRIBERY IN THE THIRD DEGREE (SUAREZ & RIOS), PROMOTING PRISON CONTRABAND IN THE FIRST DEGREE (2 COUNTS

SANCHEZ, 1 COUNT MOHAMMAD, 1 COUNT SUAREZ, AND RIOS), PROMOTING PRISON CONTRABAND IN THE SECOND DEGREE (1 COUNT MOHAMMAD)," the court secretary shouts aloud.

Everyone in the court room is flabbergasted. Ana, Antonio's mom, and Mohammad's mom are at a loss for words. Antonio feels like he's about to faint. He looks at the judge, the ADA, and everyone to see what their reactions are after hearing all the superseding counts against them. He's aware that Mya's name and Flacko's government name are in the mix. He questions their whereabouts, but they are nowhere to be found in the court room. He has a million and one questions to ask his lawyer.

Attorney Peters takes in a deep breath, "Good morning, everyone. ADA Burks and Honorable Michaels, Attorney Richard Peters here from Marksman & Sons, representing my client, Antonio Sanchez. My client would like to enter a plea of no contest, not guilty to said superseding indictment your Honor. Those pending charges have been placed in front of me and my client as they were read out to us in the court today. Is it possible to adjourn court proceedings for a later date within the next month?"

"Good morning. I would suggest you converse in detail with your client, counsel, as well as the attorney to your right and his client. Court may be adjourned for July 29th, 2014. Is that doable for all parties?"

Everyone agrees with a yes and court is adjourned for another 30 days.

Peters leans to his left and tells Antonio, "I will come speak to you about this in detail tomorrow. I did not expect this. No way should we ask for a bail reduction. I counted 19 counts on your person alone, I'll see you tomorrow."

"Ok, please. Tell my mom what's going on and that I will call her later tonight."

They return to the holding pen and are speechless. Hours pass and they return to the county jail.

THE NEXT MORNING

Peters and Antonio meet for their council visit.

"Listen, I'm a man of my word. I really can't stay here long. I have trial today for a guy facing life. I live 13 minutes form here so I came to check you. Here's your indictment paperwork. You never told me about the other two, Suarez and Rios? I found out they're your co-defendants. You won't see them ever unless we go to trial, and as far as Mohammad, even though you both are housed here, he and his attorney will probably be going to court separately from now on as well. I don't know what your rapport is with him, but just be mindful, he can offer information or flip at any time. Just like I'm telling you this, his attorney is going to advise him the same. This is just how it goes, I know this is all new to you. Next week I will bring all the discovery I can get my hands on. I explained to your mom that this is going to be a long process. It's a high profile case and corruption on Rikers and corruption in law enforcement are being looked at now more than ever. You and Mohammad are basically the poster children for what's wrong with Rikers, and the press is going to run with it. Again, sorry for the quick rundown, but I have trial in an hour. Call me in two-three days. I put $160 on the phone. Also, anything you may need to inquire about and I don't answer, tell mom or your girlfriend to call me."

Peters pauses and then continues, "I'll see you next week. Look over these charges and get an idea of what it is we can argue and fight. Also, pinpoint when and where these events occurred so I can wiggle through for argument purposes. Keep your head up, ok?

"Yes, sir. Quick question, how long you think I'm facing? Given all of this?" Antonio asks.

"Well, with a plea deal and not going to trial, I'm aiming for a 1-3years, but in all reality the lowest number on the A1 counts is eight. So that's what the judge can offer and is legally bonded to stay at, per the criminal penal law. If we take this to trial, with the 19 counts held against us, you can face 32-46 years if you are found guilty," he explains suggestively.

"Understood. See you soon, then."

They get up and shake hands.

Three weeks pass and the relationship between him and Mohammad becomes still. No love lost. Antonio even apologizes for bringing him to this madness. They keep cordial and keep close. Court day finally gets here, after going through the motions of it all. The Assistant District Attorney offers 12 years with 5 years of post-supervision. Peters denies the offer and argues that he would like to approach the judge off the record with the ADA to come to a plea bargain agreement they can both agree on. They do so in front of Judge Michaels. The ADA asks Attorney Peters if his client would be interested in a proffer, meaning he sits down in a private meeting at the DEA office with the DEA and the Department of Investigations office to give vital information on how he committed the crimes he's been charged with as well as giving information on anyone else he knows is involved in criminal activity. Peters asks the court for a 20-minute recess to speak to his client. They enter a council room and have a seat.

"Okay, so here's the deal, man. The offer on the table is 12 years, but the DA is willing to offer a proffer meeting. Basically, a meeting between you, me, the DEA, the DOI, and possibly NYPD, and all the arresting officers involved in your case. I learned that your phone has been tapped since January of this year and that your discovery is full of pictures of you making these transactions. From my professional standpoint, the guy Calbo and his friends, family, and associates were all in on this from the very beginning. If you agree with this proffer, and they get the vital information they know you have, your offer of 12 can go down extensively. You might even get offered probation and be able to avoid any prison time. You half ass it and it might only allow them to go down to that 1-3 we spoke about, or it can back fire and they don't reduce their 12 year offer. Again, the judge can offer you the bare minimum on the A1 felonies and you copout to 8 years flat with 5 years post-mandatory supervision. I need to give them an answer today or the proffer itself is retracted and off the table," Peters advises.

"So, I can't even sit on this for a few days? They basically want me to snitch on other officers?"

"Officers doing the same thing you were doing, having sexual relationships with inmates, promoting contraband. The DEA will probably ask about any illegal activity you may have knowledge about on the outside, drugs, guns, human trafficking, anything, anything they can use to help them, then they'll help you," he reminds him.

Antonio stays quiet, staring directly at him, blank.

"Remember, this stuff is sealed. It's between you and them, and you won't have to be a witness to any trial. Also, if you were to do this and go to trial yourself, you won't have this proffer held against you at trial, but I need an answer," Peters tells him.

"No, I decline it. I'm not putting my life in danger for telling on anyone. People know where my mom and sister live. I might still have to do time after this, and it's not even a definite what they'll do after I give them information. I don't like those odds at all. Tell them we decline it, sorry," Antonio respectfully informs Peters.

"Don't apologize, man. I represent you, this is your decision. Let me go out there and let them know off record that you decline. The ADA is probably going to be surprised you are declining. Court will be in another 60 days or so after this. We'll just continue to be patient and hopefully get this 12 down to eight or less, if the top charge is dropped,"

After 16 months of court proceedings and over three attempts to get Antonio to sit down with the District Attorney's office, court dates just keep getting adjourned. Peters informs him that the dragging of all this back and forth is to mentally drain Antonio and get him to talk. He advises him to keep strong. He also gets a private investigator to find out that Blanco was in fact an Undercover Drug Enforcement Agent. Calbo has been a federal informant for over 6 years pending a federal drug case along with his attempted murder case in the state. With the arrest leading up to Antonio, Mohammad, Mya and Flacko, he finagled his way to be freed from Rikers Island the same month they were all indicted. He threw them all under the bus while still selling drugs illegally under their investigation to catch them all. Loyalty meant nothing to Calbo, he had a hidden agenda from the very beginning, and the feds enabled him to still commit crimes while in prison and make drug transactions regardless.

Brandon, his brother, was also under investigation, but was allowed immunity due to Calbo's sting operation and cooperation with the DEA. Captain Davis earned his promotion through the Department of Investigations in exchange for his assistance with the investigation. He went on to be an Assistant Deputy Warden. Julissa ended up getting pregnant by Dollar after he beat trial and won a settlement against the NYPD and Department of Correction for all the years he remained incarcerated. She resigned from corrections and moved out to Miami with him. Diego was sentenced to 10 years after copping out himself. CO Garçon also was able to resign from the department after her being suspended and opened up a hair salon in Atlanta. She is making a killing.

This all transpired in the last year and a half. Antonio has been in the county jail law library heavy and educating himself of ways to cut his time. He learns about Work Release, a program for non-violent first timers like him to apply to for a chance to go home two years earlier. If all programs are completed and he maintains a clear prison record, he will have access to work in his community and get acclimated to life while still being under the supervision of corrections and earning his time through a half-way house. If he abides by all the rules and regulations, Antonio crunches the numbers and since this is a non-violent case, he also serves 5/8 of his sentence in comparison to 6/8 for violent crimes. He would end up serving 5 years, 8 months, and 21 days out of his eight year sentence. If granted the Work Release application, two years prior to his earliest release, he would be able to go home after 4 years and stay at home on the weekend. This is the goal.

Antonio is set for sentencing and Judge Michaels signals the stenograph to stop typing and goes off the record and reminds him that if he decides to go to trial the offer of 12 years can possibly go up. He is suggesting he take the 8 year minimum on the plea deal that allows him to plead guilty to A1 Criminal Possession, Conspiracy 2 & Conspiracy 4, Bribe Receiving in the 1st degree, and Promoting Prison Contraband, along with the 8 years and 5 years post-supervision.

Attorney Peters and Antonio have a brief meeting prior to taking this deal, knowing it's the best-case scenario. He does so and is sentenced 3 weeks later on April 16th, 2016. Mohammad's A1 Criminal Possession charges were dropped to an A2 due to one of his last court appearances proving the scientific reports of the narcotics lab showing he only had 36 ounces of cocaine on his person compared to the 77 ounces Antonio's duffle bag contained. Mohammad was offered 5 years and 5 years post-supervision. Flacko, being he's already an inmate of the state on unrelated charges serving 10 years, received an additional 8 years to run concurrent with this case. Mya was given 5 years felony probation due to her age and her lawyer arguing that she was coerced by her boyfriend to undergo all these acts under pressure.

2 WEEKS AFTER SENTENCING

Antonio is driven to Downstate Correctional Facility, a Maximum State Penitentiary for Reception Inmates. This is where most inmates are sent prior to arriving to their assigned prisons. Here, they are assessed by the State and given a computation sheet calculating their time and their vulnerability based on age, crime, and time of sentence. Antonio is processed by himself and placed in a room away from everyone else arriving. He's approached by a State Correction Officer and Captain.

"Sanchez, what's your date of birth?" the State CO sternly asks.

"May 30, 1988."

"The Captain wants to know if you are in fear for your life and do you request protective custody during your stay here at Downstate," the state CO tells him.

"I'm denying that request, sir," Antonio respectfully tells him.

"Listen, if we know who you are, the inmates around you will soon find out or recognize you after a while. There's a lot of foot traffic here and inmates you housed are sure to be here as well. At any time, you can notify any of my staff if you feel threatened."

"I understand fully, sir, thank you."

"You don't have to act tough. I'm suggesting you sign in protective custody for your safety, Sanchez," he sternly orders.

Antonio reminds himself of the days he would be in the law library, and that in order for him to complete programs and apply for work release he will not be able to get the incentives afforded to him if he goes into PC where he will be subjected to 23-hour lock down and 1 hour recreation away from the general population. He also reminds himself that he never did anyone wrong while working on Rikers. He was loved there and hopes the love is reciprocated in the state pen.

"I decline, sir, thank you. I will be fine in general population, trust me," Antonio tells him for the second time.

They exit the door and he gets sent to cut all his hair off, including his facial hair, which is a procedure all inmates, excluding religious reasons, have to go through. He's housed in 3-complex, and his first day a guy gets cut on his way to chow. Antonio's desensitized to that act in particular, he knows to mind his business and keep quiet.

After two months in Downstate, seeing multiple acts of violence, having visits from his mom, and getting accustomed to his surroundings as an inmate of the state and not an NYC Correction Officer, he goes through the motions very well. He gets aquatinted with a few other inmates and even sees four inmates who recognized him from Rikers. They tell him to hold it down and even send him commissary and cigarettes. There were even a few instances where Antonio received mail from inmates on Rikers who were still housed there sending him love and letters of encouragement and protection, stating that they have his back. Bloods, Crips, Trinitarios, he receives over 14 letters of recognition letting him know that no matter what facility he might end up at, he's protected. They offer their protection one, for not telling and two, for just being the well-rounded human he was. He's honored.

Antonio gets on the bus ride for transit to his designated prison. The bus ride is 8 hours long, making two stops. Mohammad is a few seats in front of him and gets off at Mid-State Prison after about a 5-hour drive. They give each other a thumbs up despite them being shackled. Antonio remains on the bus for about 3 1/2 hours longer. All he sees from now is farms and open land. The bus ride seems like forever. Finally, the bus slows down on a steep hill and out of the window he sees a 400-foot white wall.

The bus turns and one of the inmates says, "Damn, Clinton."

Antonio's heard a lot about this prison. It's a Max-A facility, two inmates actually escaped from here just one year before, and it was all over the news. He remembers 2 Pac rapping a verse about Clinton. The weather shifts from bright and sunny to dark and rainy. He prepares for it mentally with positive assurance that everything is going to be ok.

They get off the bus chained to someone in pairs. The COs here are all white. They begin screaming what's expected of them the second they sit down. The white bald-headed CO in his early 20s and covered in tattoos gets all of their attention.

"Listen up, gentlemen. This is not Downstate, this is not Rikers Island, this is not your local county! You want to be treated with respect, you give it here. You want to speak, you ask permission to! You have an issue with my staff, I personally will make it a task to make your life a living hell and you will never leave this premises, trust me! You have an issue with another inmate, you settle it in my yard! If you fight, stab, cut, or jump someone in my corridor, school, mess hall, clinic, or law library, expect repercussions by me and my staff, and it won't be pretty! Is that understood?" the white hill-billy CO shouts.

The CO looks at one of the Hispanic inmates who seems like he couldn't care less about what he's being told. "You listening to what I'm saying to you, nigger!?" the CO screams.

"With all due respect, sir, I'm not a nigger," the Hispanic inmate challenges him.

"You are definitely a nigger, inmate! You're just a nigger that knows how to swim!" he continues to belittle and scream.

They all side eye one another. Antonio realizes this is hell, just in earth form. They all grab their property and get housed. They are given an option of going to lock in their cell or go to the yard. Antonio remembers having conversations with his brother and remembers the phones are in the yard. He wants to call his mom and let her know where he is so she can send money to his account and possibly a package as soon as possible.

He walks in and the yard is huge. There's at least 300 guys out here, some on the phone, some working out at the weight pit, some playing basketball, and mostly segregated according to gang or ethnic background. He gives his ID to the officer to get assigned a slot on the phone group. The inmates around can tell the guys that just came in are new to the spot. Their state green jumpers and black boots are brand new.

Antonio does a few laps just minding his business as he knows he should. A guy from afar calls him over, a short stocky Hispanic guy, wearing a brown jacket. For it to be June, the weather is a cool 55 degrees. He introduces himself extending a fist.

"What's going on man? You just got here right?" Chino initiates.

"Yeah, a few hours ago."

"Copy, you don't bang, right?"

"Nah, I'm neutral man," Antonio reverts.

"That's a plus, man. Good for you. You smoke cigs? You want one?" Chino makes small talk.

"I'm good, brother, but thank you. I'm just waiting on my phone group to let my people know I'm here."

"I'm Chino by the way, man. If you need anything, holla at me. I'm not trying to spin you on anything, I just look out for my Latinos, you heard. Only thing I ask of you is for your paperwork tomorrow when you come to the yard. You're not a Rape-o, I could tell, but just to make sure you not a rat or anything. It's protocol here, trust me. I'll see you tomorrow. If you need shower slippers, food, I'll tell you how to go about it after, cool?"

Antonio becomes uneasy, "Yeah, I got you." Antonio walks away and hears his group number for the phone. He heads out to grab his ID. He was warned by many that this usually happens, especially in the max prison where rats, rapist, child molesters are not tolerated by neither inmates or staff. He speaks to his mom and she's relieved to hear that he's well. They plan a visit for the future even though it's an 8 hour

drive; he's 20 mins away from Canada.

THE NEXT DAY

He brings his paperwork into the yard, hidden by his sock. He read in the inmate manual book that if he gets caught with paperwork on his person and is not on his way to the law library, he can face box time. He makes sure to not ring the metal detector and face possible pat downs from staff. He sees Chino by the court and they sit alongside each other. Chino goes over his Bill of

Particulars and other paperwork. He notices quickly that Antonio was employed as a NYC Correction Officer from 2010-2014 and he reads on.

"Yo! You were a CO man? Seriously?" Chino's confused and surprised at the same time.

Antonio nods, but becomes nervous because he doesn't know how he's going to take that shocking news.

"Yeah, man. Long story, but yeah," Antonio checks his surroundings.

"Yo, this is bugged out. You're not in PC? That's what I'm surprised about. They put you in the lion's den, this is crazy, man!"

"I know. I denied it. I just want to do my programs and head out. I took 8 years," he explains.

"Wow, man, good for you. I respect this hard. I got 8 years in now, I got 12 to go. You seem like a humble dude, man. Again, anything you need, holla at me. You know where you want to work? You know how to cut hair? Or want to work in the kitchen? I do both, I can talk to my boss. You're in C-block, right?" Chino respects his entire story so much he wants to get him situated.

"Yeah, man, anything. I cut hair in county jail for a little, just got to work on my fades," he informs.

"I got you. I'm letting the guys here know that you real. Don't worry about shit. I'll give you more info on the job tomorrow. Let me go make this call, I'll see you soon. God bless you, man, for real. You should write a fucking book, a movie script, something!"

2 YEARS PASS

Antonio's been through four lock downs as a result of the inmates killing each other for gang and money and drug reasons. It gets hectic, but he remains solid. He's never had an issue with anyone here and the staff respect the way he moves along with the inmates around him. He earns his AA/NA Certificate, Floor Covering Industrial Training Vocational Certificate, he becomes a Teacher's Aide for guys earning their GED, and all while working in the kitchen at night and in the barbershop on the weekends. He keeps busy.

He starts to write the Work Release Director now that he's able to apply and they deny him twice. The first denial states he is housed in a Max-A prison making his security level high and disqualifies him. Antonio appeals that decision by proving that even though he is in Clinton, a Max-A prison, he is medium status. They reject the application for the second time saying he is not permitted to apply due to his top charge of A1 level crime. He gets into the law library and proves that his crimes are still non-violent. He appeals and gets no response back. Antonio doesn't give up and maintains his sanity by ordering screenwriting books and self-help books on publishing. He buys a portable typewriter from someone for two cartons of cigarettes that he bought from saving tips he's received cutting hair. He starts to type up a screenplay based on his story and makes himself a character in a series called "Across the Bridge - The Rikers Island Story." He creates characters based on the lives of real people, but he alters their names. Antonio dedicates any free time he has, especially when the snow and weather are unbearable.

After another year of fighting his argument, his counselor presents a letter from the Work Release Director stating he has been cleared for Work Release. Antonio made it and tells his mom over the phone that he will be home before 2019 starts, just in time for the holidays. He continues to type his book and screenplay and makes it a goal to get his story out.

He gets transferred back to the city and arrives at Lincoln Correctional Facility, a work release prison located in Harlem, New York. He made it. He fought hard to do so, but he made it. He gets plugged into a construction job and reunites with his mom, sister, and loved ones who held him down no matter what. Antonio is contacted by a publishing company who stumbled upon a podcast interview he did based on his trials and tribulations. The company offers him a book deal.

Antonio became a product of his environment with more ups and downs than a rollercoaster. All in all, God did good by him and he's turning a dark and negative situation into a light and positive one. He remains in contact with inmates he got along with through mail and pictures, giving them motivation and support.

Antonio lands a job working with the homeless under a non-profit organization that helps them with permanent housing, especially those who suffer from drug and alcohol abuse and suffer from severe mental health issues. He's a humanitarian at heart, always helping others. He went from rags to riches and back to rags, from promoting prison contraband to promoting hope.

THE END